We walked over to the edge of the pond, and six ducks swam toward us. I handed Amanda some bread to toss to the ducks.

"They're pretty friendly," I told her. "Go ahead."

One brave duck walked right up to her and took a piece from her hand just as I snapped the picture. Amanda jumped back startled and sat down on the ground.

That was when I noticed the bruise. Amanda's hair bounced up and revealed a bruise the size of a quarter in the center of her forehead. At first, I thought that she must have bumped into something. But then when I looked at it again, I saw that it was yellowing around the edges.

I tried to tell myself that little kids get bruises all the time. But I was scared. Should I tell someone? What should I do?

I Won't Leave You

by Victoria M. Althoff

To Kristen, Carrie, Cay,
and all fine, dedicated
baby-sitters everywhere

Published by Willowisp Press, Inc.
401 E. Wilson Bridge Road, Worthington, Ohio 43085

Printed in the United States of America
10 9 8 7 6 5 4 3 2

ISBN 0-87406-426-0

One

"SHE'S just about the most beautiful person I've ever seen," Anne Roberts said to me as her eyes followed every move of the woman who was carrying her tray across the lunchroom.

"Ms. Ludlow's cute, all right," I agreed. I glanced around and tried to see through the crazy blond curls of my new perm—the one nobody noticed. "She looks like one of us," I said.

Anne continued to stare at her. "I sure hope I look that good when I'm old enough to be a teacher—not that I want to be a teacher," she added as she tossed her wadded napkin at me. "I couldn't put up with girls like you, Mackenzie Tyler, who gets As on algebra tests!"

"It's just because my brother helps me study," I said. "But let's forget about when we're old. I want to look that good now."

Anne grinned. "You'll like her, Mackenzie. Ms. Ludlow is the best teacher at Brighton High."

"So you keep telling me," I said as I took a bite of my apple. "She seems terrific. But I'm worried about her photography class. You got an *A* from her last year, but she may not like me, you know?"

"That's silly," Anne said. "I promise, you'll love photography class and Ms. Ludlow. So, quit worrying about it."

Anne was a year older than me, so she had a head start at everything. I hoped that Anne was right about Ms. Ludlow's photography class. I started photography class this semester, and so far I agreed with Anne that Ms. Ludlow was lots of fun. But I didn't have much experience behind the camera lens, and I hoped Ms. Ludlow would understand.

"She doesn't talk to the class like most teachers do," I said. "She talks like she's another teenager even when she's explaining technical stuff like depth of field and shutter speeds."

"Don't you just love her hairstyle?" Anne asked me. "I wish my hair would wave that way." Anne tugged at her straight, reddish-brown hair, trying to curl it around her finger. But Anne's hair refuses to curl no matter what she does to it. I've spent a lot of sleepovers trying to make it curl, but it's impossible. Anne gave it a disgusted flick.

We were busy staring at Ms. Ludlow's hair when she turned and looked across the lunchroom at me. I felt my cheeks begin to turn red. I quickly turned back toward Anne.

"I wonder where she buys her clothes. They're cute, not like the boring clothes so many other teachers wear. I really hope that I'll do well in her class."

"All you can do is wait and see," Anne answered. "I wonder where she lives."

I grinned. "She's a teacher. Don't you know they lock them up in the supply cabinet at night? Or, maybe in Ms. Ludlow's case, she's put into a darkroom to develop photos."

"Oh, Mackenzie, I'm serious," Anne said. Anne scooted her chair back and picked up her tray.

I pushed my chair back too, but the chair leg hit something and I slammed forward. My lunch tray flew out of my hands and fell on the floor with a loud clatter. I thought my milk carton was empty, but when it bounced, little drops of white liquid splattered all over my blouse.

"Hey! Watch it!" growled a voice behind me.

"You watch it!" I yelled back as I turned around. The voice belonged to Mike Herrell, who was holding a trayful of orange juice— and I really mean a tray full of orange juice. His glass was overturned, and orange juice was running all around the hot dog that sat in the middle.

"Oops," I said, clapping my hand over my mouth.

"Nice shot, Tyler," Mike said as he walked past me.

"It's just the school lunch I've always wanted. I love hot dog à l'orange."

I winced. I would have offered to buy him something else to eat, but I only had 10 cents in my pocket. Before I could say anything, Anne held out a dollar bill to him.

"No, thanks," Mike said smiling. "I think Mackenzie has effectively killed my appetite."

"I'm sorry," I grumbled as I got up. "But you shouldn't sneak up on people."

Mike just ignored me and asked Anne why she wasn't taking photography again this year.

"I couldn't fit it into my schedule," she said, smiling up at him over the table. "Are you in the advanced class?"

"Yeah, if you can call it that," Mike said. He placed his tray with its floating food on the table beside us. I watched his serious brown eyes. "There aren't enough of us for a class by ourselves, so Ms. Ludlow stuck us in with the beginners." His gaze shifted to me for a moment before he went on. "It's okay," he said. "But it would be nicer if we had a class of our own."

It was obvious that Mike thought he was more important than beginners like me. I imagined how fun it would be to pour that orange juice mess over his head.

But my thoughts were interrupted by the click of heels coming closer. I looked up to see Ms. Ludlow walking across the lunchroom toward us. "You are just the group of people I want to talk with," she said, smiling. "Hello, Mackenzie. Hi, Anne."

Ms. Ludlow turned and looked up at Mike. Even though she wears high heels, Ms. Ludlow is only a little taller than I am. "Mike, would you be interested in covering the football game Friday?" she asked. "The *Courier* called to say that the newspaper doesn't have enough photographers to cover all of the city's high school games. They wanted to know if we'd send some pictures into them for the Saturday sports section."

Mike's brown eyes sparkled. "Sure, Ms. Ludlow. I'll be there."

Then she turned to Anne and me. "I'm glad

to see that you are in my photography class, Mackenzie. I hope you enjoy it." I always get nervous when a teacher talks to me, but I managed to stammer out an answer.

"Mackenzie, do you ever baby-sit?" The question was so unexpected that all I could do was nod.

"I was wondering if you'd be interested in sitting for my little girl on Thursday evenings while I go to my class. Why don't you think about it and see me after class today?" After another one of her bright smiles, she turned and walked away.

I knew that Anne would probably kill for a chance to sit for Ms. Ludlow's daughter. But I didn't even get a chance to say anything about it, because Mike picked up his tray again and headed back toward the trash can. I stepped forward to let him pass, but my foot caught in his chair leg just as Mike shoved the chair underneath the table.

"Ouch! Don't," I cried. Mike tugged with one hand, and I crashed into the chair. It tipped into another chair, which tipped over and hit the floor with a loud crash. I wound up on the floor.

I shook my head. I couldn't believe I was two for two on cafeteria mess-ups. "Are you okay, Mackenzie?" he asked. He put his hands on my arm to help me get up. "I'm sorry. I didn't know you had your foot caught."

I stared at his hands on my arm. His fingers were wide and warm. A tingle went down my arm to my hand. I pulled away quickly. "I'm fine. Or, I would be if you'd watch what you're doing," I said to him.

"Hey, I didn't mean to trip you," he said evenly. I watched irritation flicker in his brown eyes.

"Yeah, you don't mean a lot of stuff you do, Mike Herrell," I said. But I was just being grouchy to hide my nerves. I jerked away from him and marched out of the cafeteria.

"Wait, Mackenzie," Anne called. "What's the matter with you now?"

"I don't know," I said honestly. "I guess it's just that that guy makes me angry!"

"Who, Mike?" Anne asked. "What did he do? Why were you so rude to him just now?"

"I wasn't rude. I was just..." I protested as I looked into Anne's hazel eyes. She could usually tell what I was thinking, so I gave up my act. "Okay, I was rude," I admitted more softly. "But that guy makes me sick."

"Why?" Anne asked. "He's really nice, Mackenzie. He was in my photography class last semester."

"Yeah, and now he's in mine. But you heard

11

what he thinks of amateurs. He thinks he knows everything. You should see Mr. Know-it-all in class. Every time Ms. Ludlow wants anything demonstrated, he's the one raising his hand to do it. He's just too—"

"Self-confident?" Anne finished for me.

"He's too overbearing," I corrected her.

"Ms. Ludlow doesn't think so," Anne said pointedly. "And I think I'd be more inclined to trust her judgment on this than yours. You always make snap decisions."

"No, I don't, Anne Roberts!" I protested as Anne rolled her eyes.

"You must have a bad memory then, Mackenzie. Aren't you the one who called the police on that poor guy who was redecorating your neighbors' living room?"

I gulped. "Well, that was an honest mistake," I said. "The neighbors were on vacation, and there was a news story about criminals in a dark van who were using empty houses for drug smuggling."

"They wouldn't be smuggling drugs into Brookview, Ohio," Anne said with a giggle.

"You never know. There's always a first time," I argued, even though I knew she was right.

"Anyway," Anne went on, "how did you get so lucky? Just imagine getting to baby-sit for

Ms. Ludlow's daughter. I didn't even know she had a daughter. I wonder what her house looks like. I wonder how old her daughter is. And you, Mackenzie Tyler, are going to get to find out everything about Ms. Ludlow."

I grinned at her. I couldn't help it. I was just as excited as Anne would have been if Ms. Ludlow had asked her. Maybe I was even more excited than she would have been. A baby-sitting job was great, but a regular one was even better.

"Maybe I can earn enough money to buy that Nikon camera I saw at Morton's Photo Shop—you know, that one with all the settings." I said. "And it'll be fun getting to know Ms. Ludlow and her family."

"I guess I never really thought about her life after school," Anne was saying. "You'll have to tell me everything—just everything."

Two

"HEY, Mackenzie, how did your algebra test go?" my brother Alan asked that night at supper. He picked up his knife. "Please pass the butter, Bobbie."

Next to me at our big round table, my five-year-old sister Roberta (we call her Bobbie) was slicing thin pieces of butter from the stick. She picked them up in her fingers and carefully patterned them around the edges of her bread. "I'm not finished yet," she announced. "Wait until I'm finished."

"I got an *A*, Alan," I said. "Thanks for your help." Alan is the brain of the family, which does come in handy sometimes. He's a junior and goes to my school. "Come on, Bobbie. Everyone's waiting for some butter. You've got enough on your bread," I told her as I reached for the butter plate. But Bobbie grabbed it away from me and banged it down on the other side of her plate.

"Mackenzie! Leave her alone!" Mom said sharply. "Bobbie, put some butter on your plate, and butter your bread from that," Mom said.

Bobbie flashed an angry look at Alan and me, but she finally passed the butter.

I'd been waiting for just the right moment to tell everyone about my exciting baby-sitting job. I waited for a few minutes until everything had calmed down. But just as I was about to tell them, Alan spoke up.

"Hey, I made the varsity quiz team today," he announced proudly.

"Congratulations, I think," Dad said. "What is the varsity quiz team?"

I listened to Alan explain about how two teams compete by answering lots of questions taken from school subjects. The quiz show appears on the local TV station. The best teams at the end of the year get to compete in a big competition.

Alan is a great guy—for a brother, I mean. Anne thinks his dark hair and dark eyes make him mysterious looking. She kind of has a crush on him. But just then, I wished he'd stop talking for just a minute.

"What kind of questions will you be asked?" Mom wanted to know.

"Oh, just about everything," Alan said. "You know, stuff like art, music, history, math. You guys can come to the meets and watch. And the neatest part is that the county champions win scholarships."

I could tell that Dad was gearing up for his famous "I'm so proud of you" speech, which would mean I'd have to wait forever to talk. So, instead, I just blurted out, "Guess what? I got a job!"

"You got a what?" my father asked. His eyebrows went up.

"Well, it's just baby-sitting," I added quickly. "But it's a steady job. I'll be baby-sitting one night every week for this neat teacher, Ms. Ludlow."

Mom sat there quietly. Finally, she said, "Tell us about it, Mackenzie."

"Ms. Ludlow is my photography teacher," I said. "I think that she's the neatest teacher in the whole school. She's pretty and smart. And she talks just like one of us."

"What will she be doing during the evenings she needs you to baby-sit?" Mom asked.

"She's taking a course at Medbrook College, so she needs somebody to watch her four-year-old daughter. She said her husband works out of town and is only home on weekends. I could hardly believe it when she asked

16

me to consider taking the job."

"How late will you have to be there?" Mom asked. A sudden chill went down my back. *They couldn't tell me no, could they? This was my big chance to show how responsible I could be, and Mom sounded like I didn't know what I was doing.*

"I'll only have to be there until 9:00 when she gets home," I explained. "I can do it, can't I?"

"Of course you can, Mackenzie," Dad said with a big grin. "I'm pleased that you're so eager about it. But just remember that you've got to do it every week. It's a big commitment.

"Yeah, Mac. You can't forget where you put the kid like you do with your purse," Alan said.

I was about to kick Alan under the table, when my dad stuck up for me. "That's enough, Alan," he said. Then he smiled at me across the table. "You children definitely are growing up. Both of you need to remember that these responsibilities are honors that you must work for. When you make the decision to do these things, it's important that you live up to your end of the bargain."

It was great to hear my dad include me in his compliment speech like that. I glanced over at Mom who hadn't said anything good or bad about my job.

"Where does your teacher live?" Mom asked.

"She lives near here, I guess," I said with my mouth full. "She told me in class today that she lives on Woodbridge just across the creek." Our backyard slopes down to a little woods that edges Woodbridge Creek.

"Just remember that you cannot leave a child alone—not even for a minute," Mom added.

"Doesn't anybody want to know what *I* did today?" Bobbie asked with her lip extended in a pout.

"Tell us what you did today," I said.

Bobbie talked for the rest of dinner, telling us all about the sandbox crowd at her kindergarten. She loved going to school—and talking to everyone about it. When she gets going with her stories, it's useless to try to interrupt her.

After a few minutes, I tuned out Bobbie. I sat there and looked at my mom's expressionless face. I tried to figure out why she wasn't thrilled about my baby-sitting job. After all, I had been a good baby-sitter for Bobbie. And who could be a bigger handful than my own little sister?

I decided not to worry about it. Dad had given me his approval to baby-sit. And I would show Mom just how responsible I could be.

On Thursday night, I tucked my chin behind my wool scarf and headed outside into the windy evening. Mom and Dad had a meeting at church, so I told them I'd walk over to Ms. Ludlow's house. But her house wasn't as close to mine as it sounded, because there is a creek between the two houses. During the summertime, the creek is so low that you can practically walk across it. But during the winter, you have to walk around the creek through the neighborhood streets to reach her house.

The wind was powerful. Steady raindrops began to fall. I walked faster. By the time I reached the tall, old-fashioned house at 76 Woodbridge, the wind whipped against me, and low thunder growled in the distance. I ran up the porch steps, panting to catch my breath.

Ms. Ludlow opened the door before I even knocked. She already had on her heavy wool jacket. Her hat, gloves, and keys lay on a notebook by the door. "Come in, Mackenzie," she said cheerfully. "It's really getting cold out."

I stepped into a wide hallway where a tall piano was backed against a curved open staircase. Ms. Ludlow led me through an archway into a living room furnished in perfectly co-ordinated shades of mauve and gray. The room was beautiful and clean, though the luxurious gray carpeting was nearly covered with blocks and toy bricks.

The couch was filled with teddy bears, dolls, and tiny cars. Coloring books, crayons, and papers were strewn on the brass and glass coffee table.

"I didn't have time to straighten up," Ms. Ludlow said. "And it wouldn't do any good, anyway." She frowned, and then she added, "I hope you and Amanda have a good time to-gether."

I nodded.

"Put her to bed at 8:00. I'll be back about 9:30," she said.

I heard a giggle, but I couldn't tell where it was coming from. "Come on, Amanda. No more hide and seek. I have to leave now," Ms. Ludlow called to her.

There was another giggle. I thought the sound might be coming from the open arch-way that led to a dining room furnished with a tiny play table, kitchen set, and toybox.

"She loves to tease," Ms. Ludlow told me. "We're remodeling this house as we save up money. So, there are lots of places to hide, especially for a four year old.

"All right, Amanda. This is Mackenzie. She's the boss tonight. You be a good girl. I'll see you later. Good-bye."

Suddenly, Amanda ran past me and scampered across the room yelling, "No, no, Mommy! Mommy, don't go!"

Amanda clamped two tiny arms around her mom's slacks and cried.

Ms. Ludlow gave me an apologetic look as she bent to untangle herself from Amanda's grasp. "It's okay, honey. I have to go to my class. Mackenzie's come to play with you."

She led Amanda over to me and pried open the little fist that gripped her finger. I dropped to my knees and looked into Amanda's eyes. She began to cry again. "Don't go. Don't, Mommy!" A tear spilled from each wide blue eye and rolled down her cheeks.

"'I have to go," Ms. Ludlow apologized to me. "She used to do this and has just started again. Of course, she misses her dad, too. Ever since Dan's promotion, he has to spend the weekdays in Pittsburgh."

"We'll be all right," I said with more confidence than I felt. I took Amanda's hand and held her so that Ms. Ludlow could leave.

"No, Mommy!" Amanda wailed.

I put both my arms around the child. "It's all right. Your Mommy will be back later. Shh.

Shh." I walked with Amanda to the front window and then picked her up so she could wave through the glass.

Ms. Ludlow had left a list for me of things to do—a bath, some carrots and peanut butter for snacks, a note or two on Amanda's favorite stuffed animals to sleep with. I was impressed by Ms. Ludlow's organization. I turned to the little girl clutching my finger in her tiny fist. "Well, Amanda, I'm Mackenzie. Do you want to show me your favorite toys? Or, would you like to play hide and seek?"

Amanda's round face broke into a sunny grin. "I hide," she said. "No peeking."

It was hardly hide and seek, because Amanda wouldn't stop talking. But I pretended I couldn't hear. While I scanned the dining room in my search for Amanda, I picked up a stuffed monkey and a few blocks. I noticed a saw and some nails lying in a pile of sawdust near the doorway. I picked them up and carried them into the kitchen.

"You're not even close!" Amanda yelled from behind the sofa. "Are you looking for me?" she demanded.

"Where can Amanda be?" I asked as I placed the tools on a high shelf. "She's not in the kitchen." I came back through the swinging door, and Amanda jumped up.

"Here I am!" she called, laughing.

Then Amanda introduced me to all her dolls and teddy bears. She told me how she got each one. Finally, I helped her float sponges and boats in the tub while she soaked amidst the bubbles. When bath time was over, I was worn out.

While I sopped up the water from the bathroom floor, Amanda put on her pajamas and toddled over to the toilet. A pair of earrings lay in a dish on the sink. Amanda picked them up and dropped them into the bowl. "Going for a ride! See. They're all gone!" she said, reaching for the handle.

"Oh, no you don't, Amanda!" I cried. I dashed across the room, scooped Amanda under my arm, and carried her out. I reminded myself to retrieve the earrings as soon as Amanda was safely tucked in bed.

"Do you want a snack before bed?" I asked her.

"I'm not sleepy. Let's have snacks," Amanda said. We went down the wide stairs and into the kitchen. Dirty dishes were piled on the countertop. I figured that Amanda probably kept her mom so busy that she didn't have time to clean up. Amanda climbed onto a small chair on top of the kitchen chair, which made it higher for her. She pounded on the table. "Cookies, please," she sang.

The kitchen cupboards were nearly empty. I finally located a carrot from the bottom drawer of the refrigerator and a cookie from the jar on the countertop.

Then we went upstairs. "Let's read a story," I said. Amanda squirmed her hand out of mine. "Mandy read," she called, running toward her room. With a giant leap, she dove over the side safety bar of her bed and rummaged through the covers until she came up with a small book. But she wouldn't lie down in bed. "No bed!" she announced firmly.

Amanda showed me her "Three Little Pigs" book. "Mandy can read," she repeated.

"Okay," I agreed. I turned on the small lamp, and we sat beside the bed in a rocker. Outside, the rain began pattering against the window.

Amanda opened the book and began to tell the story in her own words. I guess that made her feel like she was reading. After a while, she settled in my arms and announced, "Mackenzie read now."

I took the book from her. But before I finished the first page, Amanda was asleep. I gently put her into bed and pulled the blanket over her. But as I started to leave, she sat up sleepily. Her eyes flickered wide and fearful. "Don't close the door!" she cried.

"Okay, I won't," I told her. I left the door open, and she lay down again.

After I cleaned up the bathroom, I washed the earrings. "Why would she leave them in here?" I asked myself.

Mr. and Ms. Ludlow's room had to be the closed door at the end of the hallway. I knew better than to snoop, but I couldn't help myself. I just had to know everything about Ms. Ludlow. I opened the door, turned on the light, and gasped. I stared at an antique carved bed—the biggest thing in the huge room. The dark wooden headboard nearly reached the ceiling. It had brass candle holders attached right to the headboard.

I padded across the thick oriental-style carpeting to the closet. Ms. Ludlow's clothes were on the left. I recognized a dress I liked. There was a green suede jumper I had never seen her wear to school. Lightning flashed outside, and rain pounded against the window. I closed the wardrobe and went to a dark wooden dresser that had an oval mirror above it.

Pictures scattered around the room showed Amanda and a tall blond man holding her. I reached for a fancy box that was sitting on her dresser. Suddenly, a huge flash lighted the whole room in brilliant white. A giant crack of thunder came right on top of it. I jumped. The box flew out of my hand and banged to the floor. I suddenly felt terrible for snooping in her things.

My hands shook as I picked up the box lid. I stared at the jumble of pins and chains inside, and then I closed it and took the earrings back to the bathroom.

Downstairs, the house felt strange and silent except for the raindrops pounding outside. I quickly washed the dishes. By the time I picked up the toys in the living room, it was nearly 9:00. I was still working on my algebra when Ms. Ludlow got home.

"It's awful out there!" she cried, as she stamped her feet on the hallway mat. Then she smiled. "Well, how did things go?" she asked me.

"Amanda's pretty active," I said with a grin. "But she's a darling." I wondered how someone could keep up with her all day long.

"I'm exhausted," Ms. Ludlow said as she dumped her notebook on the couch and plopped beside it. "I hope it went okay."

"Yes, it was just fine," I said. I got up and pulled my coat off the hook.

"I can't tell you how happy I am to have someone responsible watching Amanda," Ms.

Ludlow said as she got up. "When we lived in Milton, I used to leave her with my mother. But I've been worried about it since we've lived here." She looked into her wallet and handed me 10 dollars. I shook my head.

"I can't take that much," I protested.

"We'll agree on a rate later," Ms. Ludlow said. "For tonight, call it a bonus. I'm grateful that you could come." She peered out the window. "You'd better let me take you home."

"I'll be all right," I said, but a sudden crash of thunder made me duck.

Ms. Ludlow said, "No, Mackenzie, I insist. I can't have you catching a cold because you baby-sat for Amanda. Besides, you're very important to me." She glanced up the stairs, and then she said, "Amanda's asleep. It'll be okay to leave her for just a couple of minutes. I'll just go up and check on her. Go get in the car. It's not locked."

Ms. Ludlow dashed up the stairs while I went out to her blue sports car. As I got in and leaned against the soft seat, I thought about Ms. Ludlow and Amanda. I felt a little uneasy about Ms. Ludlow leaving her alone. What if she was awakened by the storm and got frightened? What if something happened to the house—a fire or something?

Oh well, I thought to myself. Ms. Ludlow

knew what she was doing. And Ms. Ludlow liked me. Amanda liked me. And I had 10 dollars to put toward my new camera. *Things couldn't be better*, I told myself. I could hardly wait until my parents began to notice the new, grown-up, responsible Mackenzie Tyler.

Three

"WELL?" Anne asked as we gathered our books from our adjoining lockers the next morning. She grabbed her lock and yanked on it, but nothing happened. On her third try, the lock finally opened.

I tossed my books on top of the lockers and worked my own lock combination. Then I realized that Anne had asked me a question.

"Well, what?" I asked her.

"Tell me about Ms. Ludlow," Anne insisted. "What's her house like? How old is her daughter? What does she look like? Does Ms. Ludlow have expensive furniture? What about her clothes?"

I giggled. "Which answer do you want?" I asked. It was fun to see Anne practically gasping for news about Ms. Ludlow. But I wouldn't dangle the bait for very long. Anne's lips were pressed together so tightly that I thought she would literally burst from the excitement.

"Okay, I'll tell you," I gave in. "Last night was super. Amanda is four, blond, and a darling. But boy, is she active! I don't think I stopped running after her all night."

"What about Ms. Ludlow's house?" Anne asked eagerly.

I told her all about the beautiful living room and dining room. I wanted to tell her about Ms. Ludlow's bedroom with the antiques, but Anne interrupted my thoughts.

"Just tell me the good stuff," she said. "You know, like about her clothes and stuff she has in her closets."

I stuck my nose in the air. "What makes you think that I'd snoop?" I asked in mock horror.

"Don't tell me you didn't look around her house. I would, and I know that you would, too. I mean, you're the kind of person who eavesdrops on supposed spies at the discount store and then calls the CIA."

"Aren't you ever going to let me forget that?" I asked. I could feel my face turning red.

"It's too great a story to forget, even if you were only 10 at the time, Mac." Anne chuckled.

"All right," I relented. "Yes, everything at

Ms. Ludlow's house is beautiful. She has this terrific antique bedroom with a bed head-board that almost reaches the ceiling. It's all carved wood and gorgeous. She lives a really elegant life, and she's so organized. Oh, she also has this spectacular green suede dress."

I stopped talking, because Anne's eyes were making weird expressions. She seemed to be focusing on something behind me. "What's up?" I asked, starting to turn around to see what she was looking at.

"Don't bother looking," Anne told me. "It's your orange juice gourmet."

"I've been trying to avoid him ever since the other day," I whispered. "I don't know what made me yell at him like that."

"Well, good old Mike Herrell is heading our way," Anne said. "You better get ready for the next confrontation."

"Let's just get out of here and pretend that we don't see him," I said. I slammed my locker shut. The latch didn't close and the door bounced back at me.

"Hey, Mackenzie," Mike called.

"Oops, it's too late. I'll leave you two alone," Anne said with a mischievous grin. Then she walked down the hall.

"Come back here, you coward," I called after her. She just ignored me.

I gulped and turned around. Mike was standing just inches away from me. I took a step backward. "Uh, hi, Mike," I said uneasily.

I couldn't figure out why my hands and voice both seemed shaky. I knew I should apologize to him for the other day. But instead we just stood there staring at each other.

"I'm sorry that..." we both began at the same time. Then we both grinned.

"Uh, you go first," I said.

"No, I didn't mean to interrupt," Mike said.

I looked up at him. I'd never noticed before that Mike's eyes had warm dark flecks in the middle or that he was so tall. Then I realized that I was staring at him. *Okay, Mackenzie, get this over with.* I opened my mouth, but nothing came out.

"I wanted to say that I'm sorry for being upset at you the other day," Mike said.

"No, I'm sorry," I said in a rush. "I shouldn't have lost my temper like that."

"Well, I should have let you know that I was behind you," Mike said as if he hadn't heard me.

"No," I argued. "I need to watch what I'm doing. Besides, I shouldn't have yelled at you."

"I guess I must have sounded pretty rude

griping about being in the class with beginners," Mike said.

"Well, yeah, you did," I admitted. "But I guess I can understand your point. You have already learned everything and we're just beginning."

Mike grinned down at me. His cute smile made me giggle.

He extended his hand to me. "That's enough apologizing all around," he said.

"Okay," I said as I shook his hand. We stood there awkwardly for a minute, and then I picked up my books.

"Are you on your way to photo class?" Mike asked.

I nodded, and we started walking down the hall together. "This is my favorite part of the day. Ms. Ludlow is so—" he began.

"Cool," I finished for him.

"Yeah, that's the word," he said. "Last year at the middle school, there wasn't a photography class. But Ms. Ludlow offered to come over to the school and talk to any kids who were interested. And before the year was up, we had taken some pretty neat photos. We even entered some in the *Brookview Courier*'s spring photo contest. We didn't win, but it was fun."

"Had you taken many pictures before

meeting Ms. Ludlow?" I asked him.

He shrugged. "Not really. I just got my first camera last year."

As we walked into the classroom, I said, "Thanks for not being upset with me."

Mike gave me a strange look. "I thought you were the one who was upset with me."

I laughed. "Well, I tend to say things that I don't mean."

Mike chuckled. "I'll remember that the next time you give me a compliment."

"Not that I ever would," I teased. I was still smiling as I sat down in my seat.

Ms. Ludlow was wearing the green suede dress I saw in her closet. Her dark brown hair seemed to glisten in the sunshine that streamed in the side window.

"I know that you've heard a picture is worth a thousand words. Well, a picture won't tell you anything unless you plan for it to," she explained. "Today, we're going to begin learning how to plan your photos to tell the story that you want. Photos tell your story as no one else can. It's a very personal thing."

I watched Mike who was sitting across the room. He was listening intently to Ms. Ludlow's discussion of last week's assignment. That brought me back to reality. I had forgotten all about the assignment.

"...a series of pictures that tell a story or create a scene," she was saying. "They will make up your photo essay." She held up a series of framed photos. "These were Mike Herrell's essay last year in middle school," she said, which made a bunch of kids turn around to stare at Mike. He was blushing. When I caught his eye, he gave me an embarrassed grin.

"Notice the way that Mike used light in this series of photos. He featured the boats at the landing," Ms. Ludlow explained. "Along with the changing activity, the angle of light shows the passage of time."

She displayed the photos against the chalkboard while she gave us deadlines to complete the project. I kept looking at Mike's pictures. His photos began in the morning with the bustle of fishing boats and people gathering their gear for the day. Then they featured the emptiness of the day, followed by a few people doing repairs in the afternoon. The final photo showed everything tucked in and tranquil for the night. Ms. Ludlow was right—it told a whole story.

Just as the bell rang, Ms. Ludlow called out, "Mackenzie Tyler, may I see you for just a moment?"

My heart began beating faster. It always

does when a teacher calls on me. The class filed out before I was able to catch my breath. I kept remembering how I had sneaked into her bedroom last night, and my legs were shaky as I walked up to her desk.

Ms. Ludlow was flipping through her grade book. It made me nervous just to watch her. "Mackenzie," she said with a big smile. "I want to ask you for a big favor."

When I couldn't find my voice, she went on. "We've been wanting to set up a photo lab here, with a darkroom and a couple of enlargers so everybody who wants to can learn to develop and print pictures. The principal has agreed that it's okay."

I nodded, but I didn't know what that had to do with me. Then she said, "I need to stay today until 5:00 to present the idea to Mr. Jarvis and a couple of people from the school board. Anyway, Amanda's due to be picked up at her day care at 4:00. I know this is short notice, but I wondered if you could pick her up and walk her home?"

I must have looked surprised, because she hurried to say, "The center's only a block away. And I can be home by 5:30."

"Sure, Ms. Ludlow. I'd be glad to help out."

Ms. Ludlow smiled. "That's wonderful, Mackenzie. I'll call the center. Here's the address. You just turn right at the corner of the schoolyard and walk straight down the street." She paused. "Oh, you'll need to call home, too, I expect, to let your parents know."

We walked to the office to make our calls. "Give Amanda a snack if she wants one," Ms. Ludlow was saying. "I think there are the little pizzas that she likes in the freezer."

I barely heard her. I kept thinking what a stroke of luck this was. I could hardly believe it. It was only for an hour, and it was money that I could use to buy a camera. Somehow, talking with Mike today and looking at his pictures made me really want to learn photography.

Maybe Mike would help me. Suddenly, I felt my face get hot as I realized how fast that daydream had popped into my head. This is not the time to be thinking about a guy you barely know, Mackenzie Tyler. Quickly, I turned my thoughts back to Ms. Ludlow as we walked into the office.

Four

THE Kid Connection Day Care Center was in a large old house on Mill Street, just a block from the school. Ms. Ludlow told me that she had picked that day care because it was nearby in case of an emergency.

I walked up the stairs to the porch, wondering if Amanda would remember me. What if she refused to leave with me? What if she cried? I rang the door bell, and a petite, gray-haired woman with a kind smile opened the door.

"Hello," she said.

"I've brought this note from Ms. Ludlow giving me permission to take Amanda home," I explained.

"You must be Mackenzie Tyler," the woman said.

I nodded.

"I'm Mrs. Goodman," the woman said.

"Won't you come in? We think Amanda is a delightful child. She is so bright."

I found Amanda busily organizing the pots and pans in a child-sized play kitchen. She was talking to herself.

When Amanda saw me, she yelled, "Mackie!" She dropped a pan and ran to me at full speed. So much for whether she would remember me. Together, we put away all the kitchen toys. Then Mrs. Goodman handed me Amanda's coat and helped her snuggle into it.

Amanda happily charged outside and down the stairs, pulling me after her. "Do you want to play at the park?" I asked her. "It's on our way home."

"Yes, the park," Amanda chattered happily. "Swings. I love swings."

She led me across the wide grassy playing fields toward the small children's area. She climbed into a swing seat, and waited for me to push her. She giggled the whole time. Then I helped her onto a hobby horse. We ended the afternoon with a couple of rides down a big sliding board.

After all that, I was exhausted. I bent over to tie Amanda's shoe laces, and suddenly I heard a familiar voice behind me.

"Well, if this isn't the last place I'd expect

to see you, Mackenzie."

I could feel my face turning red. I mean, what a graceful position to be in when someone comes up behind you.

"Hi, Mike!" I called over my shoulder.

Mike came over to stand behind me. "Is this your sister?" he asked.

"No, this is Amanda Ludlow," I said. "Amanda, this is Mike."

"Mackie," Amanda repeated. "Can I swing?"

"All right, Amanda. You can swing again," I said as I stood up. "What are you doing here, Mike?"

"I had basketball practice," he said. "But it was called off today. Is this Ms. Ludlow's daughter?"

I nodded as Amanda ran toward the swings. "She's wearing me out. I'm not sure it was such a good idea to stop here."

"Can I help?" Mike offered.

"That's really nice of you, but you don't have to," I said.

"I know I don't. But I think it'd be fun," he said. "Besides, with two people, it will be easier to deal with a little kid."

We walked over to where Amanda sat patiently on the swing. Mike stooped and shook hands with her like she was an adult. "Hi, Amanda. I'm Mike. Would you like me to push you?" Mike asked gently.

Amanda nodded.

"Now hold on tight!" He pushed and Amanda squealed happily as the swing moved forward.

"Have you started your photo project yet?" Mike asked as he pushed.

I shook my head. "What about you?"

Mike shrugged his shoulders. "Well, I did take three rolls of film, but I didn't get anything I liked out of it," he admitted.

"I thought you were the expert," I teased.

"I'm far from being an expert. Of course, now that I told you about my terrible pictures, yours will probaby be wonderful."

"Yeah, I'll just bet," I said, giggling.

"You could even get a nice series of photos with Amanda here," he suggested.

I frowned. "I don't know if Ms. Ludlow would allow that," I said.

Mike tilted his head. "You could ask her," he suggested. "The key is to not be discouraged with your first pictures," he said. "When I got my new camera, I took a bunch of completely horrible photos. I thought I was being so creative, and they just looked stupid instead. I was ready to take the camera back and buy a bicycle."

"You thought of doing that?" I asked. "But

you're so talented at taking pictures."

Mike smiled. "Well, I wasn't then. Just don't give up. If I can learn to use a camera, you can, too. And with the new photo lab being set up, we'll learn to do everything from developing to enlarging and printing. I can hardly wait."

"How's the lab coming?" I asked him.

"Oh, it's slow, but we're getting there. Why don't you stop in after school someday? We all have a lot of fun working on it."

"It sounds great," I admitted. I would try to stop by after school soon.

Amanda had lost interest in swinging. Mike put her down, and we walked with her between us to Woodbridge Street. We didn't get a chance to say anything more, because Amanda chattered the whole way. When we got to the corner, she broke away from us and ran down the street toward home. "I'll see you later," I called to Mike. "Right now, I've got to keep up with her." Then I called to Amanda, "Hey, Amanda, wait for me."

It always seemed to be my luck. Whenever I got into an interesting conversation with a guy, I was interrupted. As I ran after Amanda, I realized that there was so much to learn about Mike Herrell. Every time I had a conversation with him, it seemed like there was something new to hear about.

Today, I had seen Mike's gentler side. The way he had played with Amanda was really sweet. After the orange juice episode, I never would have believed that Mike could be so nice. I finally caught up with Amanda and grabbed her hand as we crossed the street. I unlocked the front door and then turned to wave to Mike, but he was already walking the other way.

Amanda kept repeating that she was hungry, so I did a quick search of the kitchen cupboards and the refrigerator. I couldn't find any of the little pizzas that Ms. Ludlow had mentioned, but I finally found some stale crackers for Amanda to eat.

While Amanda crunched, I read her a story. We sat together in the rocker until Ms. Ludlow got home. I felt kind of shy about asking Ms. Ludlow to use her daughter as my photo subject, but she seemed to think it was all right. "What a compliment," she told me. "What type of camera will you be using?"

"I'll probably use my instamatic," I said.

"You'll need a camera that stops action," Ms. Ludlow said as she walked over to the hallway closet. She reached high up on the shelf while she talked. "Amanda's pretty active. You said so yourself. So, I keep my old 35 millimeter camera up here."

Ms. Ludlow took the camera down and handed it to me. "Here, use this one of mine," she said.

I could hardly believe it. "Thank you," I said over and over as I got ready to leave.

During my walk home, I pictured myself with a real camera taking great pictures like Mike does. But when I walked into our house, I heard my mom talking to someone. "I don't know. Mackenzie is a little young for that kind of responsibility."

My ears began to burn. I was upset. Who was she telling about my irresponsibility now? I dumped my books on the living room sofa and went to the kitchen to get a glass of milk.

If my mother could have seen me picking up Amanda after school and playing with her at the park, she wouldn't be talking about me like that. I got Amanda home safely, and I even found her a snack when hardly anything was in the cupboards. As I reached into the refrigerator, the swinging door to the hallway opened, and Mother leaned into the room, still talking over the telephone.

"Oh, Mackenzie has just gotten home. Would you like to speak with her? Okay, hold on." Mom covered the mouthpiece. "It's Ms. Ludlow, honey. Here."

A funny lump bobbed its way into my throat as I took the phone from her. Why would Ms. Ludlow be calling when she just saw me? Did she want her camera back? And why was my mother calling me irresponsible?

"Hello?" I said into the phone.

"Mackenzie," Ms. Ludlow said, her voice hurried. "I wanted to clear it with your mother before asking you, but would you be interested in baby-sitting for Amanda every afternoon after school? You did such a great job today that it would be such a help to have you every afternoon. That way, I could use the time to get the new lab set up."

I gulped. The idea of making extra money was terrific, but I really did want some free time to get to know Mike better.

Ms. Ludlow paused, and when I didn't say anything, she went on talking. "You see, I got the final okay to set up the photo lab, so it looks like I'm going to have to stay late every day for a while. I don't like to leave her in day care after all her friends have left. And, besides, Amanda likes you a lot. I do, too."

I smiled at that. I said, "It sounds fine, Ms. Ludlow. I'd love to do it."

My mind was racing. I really wanted to baby-sit just on Thursday nights, but I was worried that it was all or nothing. If I said no, maybe she'd give the whole job to somebody else. I didn't want to risk that.

Ms. Ludlow thanked me, and I hung up. I couldn't stop grinning. Anne was going to be so jealous. I couldn't wait to call her. The camera I had dreamed about buying would soon be mine.

I started upstairs, then I started thinking about Amanda. She was so adorable, but she was demanding at the same time.

"But I can handle it," I told myself out loud. Then, maybe people will believe that I can handle responsibility.

"Mackenzie," my mother called from the living room, "come take your books upstairs."

I gulped and turned around.

Five

I didn't expect to enjoy baby-sitting every day after school. I don't know exactly what I had expected—maybe just to make a little money toward my camera.

Some afternoons as Amanda and I walked toward her house, I held her hand and she told me all about the kids in her pre-school. I began to feel like I knew Tommy, Heather, and Betsy, too.

Amanda definitely was a talkative little girl. At times, she ran ahead of me yelling, "Catch me! Catch me!" Then, just as I would yell for her to stop running, she'd skid to a halt at the corner.

That first week, we stopped to play at the park several times. I pushed Amanda on the swings or watched her slide down the slides. I always waited for her at the bottom of the slide, and she giggled when I caught her.

I watched for a chance to take some cute pictures of Amanda, but she hardly stood still long enough for me to take the camera from my pocket. She was so full of energy that I was worn out before we got home. On our way home every day, we raced from the corner of Woodbridge and Highland down the two blocks to the Ludlows' front door. That is, Amanda raced, and her blond curls bobbed in the late afternoon sunlight. I made sure to run along behind her so I could watch her.

When we got home, I always tried to find Amanda a snack. I say that I tried to, because often Ms. Ludlow had very little food in the house. Sometimes, she suggested something for me to fix, but when I looked through the cupboards, there wasn't any food there. I figured that she was so busy that she just didn't pay any attention. After all, she was late getting home two nights the first week.

I convinced Amanda to help me pick up her toys. I let her know what a big girl she was for being responsible and helping out. We made it into a game. I put on one of Amanda's records, and we both ran around the room trying to see who could get the most things into the toybox before the record ended. Amanda loved it.

But just like a little kid, whenever we had

the house looking great, Amanda would drag stuff back out again. When I arrived at the house each day, her toys would be scattered everywhere.

One afternoon, just as we finished cleaning up and rearranging all the toys in special nets that hung on the walls, the clock in the living room chimed, signaling that it was 5:00. I brought out one of Amanda's favorite toys, and we sat down to wait for Ms. Ludlow. At 5:30, I figured we'd better do something to keep Amanda busy or she'd begin to yell for dinner.

When Ms. Ludlow finally got home at 5:45, Amanda and I were sitting on the sofa reading a book together. I stood up to see her face when she noticed how we'd cleaned up all the toys. Amanda sat quietly, flipping through her book. Finally, she put it down and walked toward her mother.

Ms. Ludlow didn't even notice what we'd done. She hurried through the living room, hung her coat in the closet, and walked back into the room with a big smile on her face.

"Guess what, girls?" she said excitedly. "I've been given the chance to take the photographs for a new textbook!"

"Mommy!" Amanda shouted. She clamped her arms around her mother's knees.

"That's wonderful," I said.

"I stopped over at the college to pick up my project, and Professor Wilson was there. He's writing a new astronomy textbook, and he needs pictures of stars. He also liked the night pictures that I took of the freeway and my time exposure of the North Star. Wait'll you see it, Mackenzie."

She pulled Amanda's hands away from her legs, dropped her backpack on the couch, and opened a large portfolio. Then she rummaged through it and found her picture. It was black, with circles of white lines streaked around a center point as if the image was spinning.

I stared at her photograph as Ms. Ludlow explained that the North Star was in the center of the photo. By angling the camera and setting her camera for time exposure, she showed the circular rotation of earth. The streaks were the movement other stars seemed to make as the earth turned below them.

"Congratulations," I told her. I was a little disappointed that she didn't notice our cleaning job. I was also worried that I was late getting home. I started walking toward the coat rack as Ms. Ludlow continued talking.

"It's a great opportunity because if the publisher uses my photos, I may get more work from them," Ms. Ludlow said.

"That's great," I said.

"Or, I may get other clients," she added enthusiastically. "It might not be too long before I can start my own studio."

"Uh, that's wonderful," I agreed, but this time I marched to the coatrack. "I have to get home now," I said. "Bye, Amanda. I'll see you tomorrow."

As I left the house, I looked up at the darkening sky. "Mom is not going to like this," I said to myself. I decided to take the shortcut between our houses. I walked around the Ludlow house and down through the sloping yard to the woods.

The darkness seemed to close in around me. My feet crunched loudly in a thick layer of crisp fallen leaves. I stumbled under low branches and pulled past the clinging shrubs. I'm not usually afraid of the dark, but there was something eerie about the woods.

I was glad when I got to the creek, because the gurgling water was comforting. I climbed onto a fallen log, and scrambled across. I was so happy to get to the woods on my own side that I ran up the slope, crashing into bushes as I went. I stopped at the foot of our yard to catch my breath. That was when I heard it—a snuffling, rustling sound. Something else was moving in the bushes beside me. It moved closer. I froze. It moved again. I ran.

I pushed so hard on the back door that it flew open. I stumbled inside into the warmth of the kitchen. "I'm home!" I called, but I was panting and my heart was thudding hard against my chest.

"It's about time," Mom said. She gave the chili a stir and lifted it from the burner. She turned around and put her hands on her hips. "I was worried about you," she said.

I gulped. "I didn't expect Ms. Ludlow to be so late," I explained.

"Well, next time, please call to let me know," she said. "Now let's eat. I'm sure you're starved."

"Yes, I am." I mentally kicked myself for not remembering to call. I was so proud of rearranging all of Amanda's toys that it hadn't occurred to me to call home. I had been so concerned with keeping Amanda happy that I'd forgotten to be responsible with my family, too. I grabbed some silverware and walked into the dining room to set the table.

"I'm glad you're handling the responsibility of your job so well, Mackenzie," Mother said as she brought in bowls of chili. "I know it's hard to do anything else when you're watching Amanda. Is the job making it hard for you to do your homework?"

"No, I'm doing just fine," I said absently as I placed the forks.

"Well, what about activities? I haven't seen Anne around here for a couple of weeks."

That made me think about the photo lab that Mike had talked about. But then I reminded myself that I really was enjoying taking care of Amanda. And I was still surprised that my parents let me decide to take on the job. Last year, when I wanted to start a dog-bathing business, my mother had said a flat "no."

"Well, Mackenzie, I sure hope you like that little girl. I missed my biggest rooter at the after-school meet today," Alan said as he walked into the dining room.

He grabbed a hot pad and pulled the corn bread out of the oven. I suppose I frowned at his remark, because he said quickly, "I didn't mean that sarcastically. I just meant that I missed you there today, that's all. Can't a brother be mushy without his sister getting upset?"

"Tell me all about it, Alan," I said.

"We tied. We have to meet Winston in a rematch next week," he said.

"Don't worry, Alan," I said. "You'll do just fine. I bet you win the championship this year.

And I promise to come to the semifinals. They're in the evening, right?"

"Yeah, and I'll consider that a promise," Alan grinned as he popped my head with the hot pad. "Now, let's eat."

After dinner, Anne called. "I hardly ever see you anymore," she complained. "You take off after school, so we don't get to walk together anymore. And the last two times I called you, you were baby-sitting."

"I know," I told her. "But I can't do anything about it. Ms. Ludlow needs me to help out with Amanda, and I already agreed to do it."

I could almost hear Anne wrinkle her nose over the phone. "Well, I miss you. But I guess you know now that I told you the truth, right?"

"About what?" I asked.

"Ms. Ludlow is a terrific lady."

I thought about that. Ms. Ludlow always was organized for class. She made the kids work hard and feel wonderful about their projects. But at the same time she never seemed to have the right snacks for Amanda. And she hadn't even noticed when we reorganized the toys in her living room.

"Well, isn't she?" Anne demanded. I knew Anne didn't want to hear anything else, so I just agreed. I told Anne that I had lots of school work to do and we hung up right after that. I tried to tell myself that Anne was right about Ms. Ludlow. But I couldn't shake the feeling that there was something wrong somewhere.

I had just sat down to begin my homework when Mike called. I practically fell off my chair when I heard his voice. The only other boy who had ever called me was Bobby Turnbull, but that was in third grade. And he was just angry because I set his frog loose.

Mike said, "I thought you might like to know we're getting our enlargers in the lab tomorrow. Maybe you could stay and help set them up."

"Thanks, Mike. It sounds like fun, but I can't," I said. "I have to baby-sit for Amanda Ludlow."

"Do you do that all the time?" he asked.

"Yes, just until Ms. Ludlow gets home after school," I said.

"Oh, I didn't realize that. I guess if Ms. Ludlow is at school after hours, then someone has to be watching out for Amanda."

Mike sounded so disappointed that I really wished I could help with the lab. I remembered Mother's words about my job interfering with my social life. I didn't say anything, so Mike asked me about my project.

"Did you decide to do your photo series on Amanda?" he asked.

"Well, I keep thinking that I will, but every time I'm with her, she keeps me so busy that I haven't been able to take pictures," I told him. "I guess I've got to find another subject."

"Maybe you just need another pair of hands," Mike suggested.

"I must need something," I agreed.

"Well, I have to stay to help with the enlarger tomorrow, but Wednesday I could come. Amanda knows me. I could keep her busy while you take pictures. Do you want to try it?"

"Mike, you're a lifesaver," I said. "That is really nice of you."

"Don't mention it," he said. "I think it'll be fun."

We talked a little more, and then he said, "There's one more thing. The museum is having a one-day show on the history of photography. I think it's a traveling exhibit. It's only here on Saturday. Do you want to go?"

My stomach gave a little flip that sent my heart spinning up to my throat. My hands felt clammy against the receiver. I couldn't believe that I could get so nervous so fast.

"Sure, Mike. I'd love to go."

Six

I patted the camera in my pocket as I walked into the Kid Connection on Wednesday. I had two rolls of film, and I'd spent last night practicing with the depth of field and shutter speeds on Ms. Ludlow's camera.

I was excited that Mike had agreed to help with my project. He was going to meet me at the park as soon as he finished with the enlargers. He'd done most of the work already, but there were a few last finishing touches.

I spotted Amanda sitting quietly at a large table. She was drawing large splotches of red, yellow, and black spots on a big sheet of white paper.

"Mackie!" she called when she saw me. "See my sun?" She pointed to her messy yellow splotch.

"That's beautiful, Amanda," I told her. I bent down to see her work. "And what's this?"

I pointed to the red and black scribbles.

Amanda shook her head as if she didn't know. But then she answered softly, "A bad door. That's a bad door."

I had no idea what she was talking about. So, instead I got her coat from the wall hook, and we headed outside. I helped her into her coat and she ran off ahead. I had to jog to keep up with her.

"Do you want to go the park, Amanda?" I asked. "I'd love to take your picture." She bobbed her head.

"Swing and slide," she said. As soon as we got to the park, she ran over to the springy horses. She loved to bounce up and down on them. Next I caught her as she came down the slide. I began to wonder if Mike really was coming.

"Catch me, Mackie!" Amanda yelled. She came shooting down the slide, but this time I wasn't ready. She ran smack into me. "Oof!" I gasped. That was when I heard a familiar voice behind me.

"Well, I see you found something to do while I was struggling with electrical cords."

I caught my breath and answered, "Hi! Boy, am I glad to see you."

Mike came over beside me. "Hello, Amanda. Do you remember me?" he asked.

"Hi," Amanda said. "Want to swing now?"

"Oh good, Mike. She remembers you!" I said.

"How can I help?" Mike asked me.

"I'm not sure," I said. "You could push her while I try to take pictures."

We followed Amanda over to the swings. Mike picked her up and helped her onto the seat.

"Remember to hold on tight, Amanda," he said as he pushed.

Amanda giggled.

I got out the camera and tried a straight-on shot with the swing coming toward me.

Mike cleared his throat, and I looked at him. "Do you mind a suggestion or two?" he asked.

I nodded. "This is my first time to use the camera and my first photography class. All suggestions are welcome."

"Well, try stooping to the same level as the swing for a straight-on shot like that," Mike instructed. "You could also try shooting up from the ground. That way you take the photo from Amanda's perspective. You know, the photo will reflect the way Amanda sees the world."

I tried Mike's suggestion. I also photographed Amanda on the horses, the slide, standing on the monkey bars with Mike holding her ankles, and running through the grass. The camera was so unfamiliar to me that I could only hope some of the pictures would come out all right.

We walked toward home with Amanda between us. "Do you want to see the ducks, Amanda?" I asked her as we passed by the neighborhood pond.

Six mallards were swimming in the pond. When we walked over to the water's edge, they swam over to us. I gave Mike the loaf of bread that I'd brought along, and we showed Amanda how to toss it to the ducks.

"Greedy, aren't they?" Mike asked as they scrambled for the bread.

"They're pretty tame," I said. "I feed them all the time. Other people do, too."

One brave duck walked right up to Amanda and took a piece of bread from her hand just as I snapped the picture. Amanda jumped back, startled, and sat down on the ground. I got a picture of that, too.

That was when I noticed Amanda's bruise. Her hair bounced up and revealed a bruise about the size of a quarter. It was right in the center of her forehead. At first, I thought that she must have bumped into something. But then when I looked at it again, I saw that it was yellowing around the edges.

Mike quacked at the ducks, and Amanda began to quack, too. I took another picture, reminding myself that little kids always manage to bruise themselves. I mean, Bobbie falls down all the time.

Ms. Ludlow got home just as I was unbuttoning Amanda's coat. Amanda crawled up on the couch and lay down.

"So, did you get any good pictures?" Ms. Ludlow asked cheerfully.

I wrinkled my nose. "Mike Herrell came over and helped me today. It was just about impossible to take pictures of Amanda without another person there to help take care of her."

Ms. Ludlow nodded. "That's true. I'd forgotten. Dan and I used to get lots of pictures of her, but now that he's gone all week..." She turned to Amanda. "Hello, little lady. Do you want a snack, or shall we just wait for supper?"

Amanda looked up, but didn't answer. "We must have worn her out with the fresh air and the swings," I said.

"Good," Ms. Ludlow said smiling. "That'll give me a chance to get organized. Sometimes, all I do at home is chase Amanda."

"I know what you mean. How's the photo lab coming along?"

"Oh, it's going well," Ms. Ludlow said

enthusiastically. "We got the enlargers finished today. I have a friend who's offered to donate several used developing trays from his studio. There's just a little more left to do before we can begin developing all our own photos."

"I'm sorry I can't help," I said.

"You're more help than you can imagine," Ms. Ludlow told me. "It's wonderful to know that Amanda is in good hands so that I can stay at school and work with the kids."

I beamed under her complimentary smile, but I still wished I could help with the lab.

As Ms. Ludlow turned to hang up her coat, she said, "At least the kids at school appreciate what I do." Then she crossed the room and handed me an envelope. "This is for this week's baby-sitting, Mackenzie. Tomorrow, I've planned to go directly from school to my class, so I've included a little extra for that."

I must have looked startled, because Ms. Ludlow added, "Amanda always makes such a scene when I leave that I thought it would be less traumatic all around that way. You won't mind fixing some supper for yourself and Amanda, will you? I'll leave something for you to make."

"No, I don't mind," I said.

As I walked home, I thought again about

my mom's comments about my free time. I didn't think she'd be too thrilled that I wouldn't be home for dinner tomorrow. But the generous check that Ms. Ludlow gave me certainly made it worth the extra time. And I really had grown fond of Amanda.

But when I got home, I was right. My parents weren't crazy about the idea.

"Mackenzie, you might need a break between taking Amanda home in the afternoon and sitting with her in the evening," Mom said during dinner.

"Or Amanda might need a break from you," Alan teased.

I didn't say anything.

"That's enough, Alan," Dad said. "This is a serious question." He turned to me. "Your mother and I have begun to worry about the amount of time you spend baby-sitting Amanda, Mackenzie."

"I'm getting my schoolwork done okay, Dad," I said.

"It's not your homework that we're concerned about," Mom added. "You're not seeing your friends at all. And you never get a chance to just rest, watch television, or go shopping."

I couldn't believe that Mom was concerned about my free time. For as long as I could remember, my parents had bugged me to show some responsibility—like Alan does. But now that I'd gotten a great baby-sitting job, my parents were worried about shopping and friends. What did they want from me?

"I'm fine, Mom," I said, but I knew she wasn't going to let the subject drop there. When Mom and Dad agreed on something, they wouldn't let it go that easily. But I didn't want to give up my job. I was too close to earning the money for a camera of my very own. And, besides, who would take care of Amanda?

"Mackenzie, you don't realize how difficult it is to cook and watch a four year old at the same time," Mom was saying.

Before I could say anything, my dad started in. "Four years old is a dangerous time in a child's life. At that age, children think they can do anything, and they're likely to try it. She could get into trouble in a matter of seconds."

"But, Dad, Ms. Ludlow barely has time to get from school to the college. If she has to come home first, she may not get to her class on time." I glanced at my father and quickly added, "Besides, you're always telling me to be more responsible. Now that I have a good job, do you want me to quit?"

Dad shook his head. "I don't want you to quit, honey, but I do want you to be aware of two things. Fixing dinner for Amanda is not like getting an apple from the refrigerator for yourself. You have to keep her within your sight, but away from the stove."

"I know that, Dad," I said.

"If she leaves the room, you have to go after her," he said. "You can't leave her on her own."

I nodded.

Dad said, "I guess I keep remembering that awful tragedy a couple of months ago when that child was burned while playing with matches. His mother had just gone next door to pick up a package from the neighbor."

"Honest, Dad. I am careful with Amanda."

"I know. We both worry about you too much, I guess," Dad said. "I am proud of the way you've taken charge of your job. But I do want you to have fun in your life, too."

"You could ask your teacher to get someone else for part of the time," Mom suggested. "Or, maybe she could stay late only on certain days."

I frowned, but Mom ignored me. "And why don't you suggest cold meals to her as an alternative to cooking for Amanda? Or, maybe she could have a casserole ready for you to slip into the oven."

"That's a great idea," I said. But somehow I knew that the ideas would never work well with Ms. Ludlow.

Seven

ON Thursday night, I tried a dozen ways to get Amanda to play quietly in the kitchen while I warmed some soup for supper. I gave her some crayons and paper and sat her at the table, but she jumped up before I even got the can open. I followed her into the living room where she climbed on the sofa and stared out the window.

"Amanda, come into the kitchen with me so I can fix you some soup."

"I want to go outside," Amanda demanded.

"You can't go out right now. But if you let me get our supper made, I'll take you outside later, okay?" I tried to reason. "Why don't you get a book and read to me in the kitchen?"

While I put the soup into the saucepan and found mugs, crackers, and spoons for us, Amanda "read" me a garbled version of the Gingerbread Man. Then she mumbled, "Pigs.

Pigs. I'll get my pigs." She shoved the swinging door to the dining room open and ran. I was about to chase her when I glanced at the stove and saw the soup boiling over the top of the pan. I ran to turn the burner off. Then I sopped up the boiled over soup with a paper towel. It was then I notice that I couldn't hear Amanda's voice.

"Amanda!" I called. "Where are you?"

I put the pan back on the burner and went to look for her. She wasn't downstairs. I called several times as I ran up to her room. She wasn't there, either. I ran through the upstairs hallway, flinging doors open. "Amanda! Are you hiding?" I yelled. There was only silence. I stopped in the upstairs hallway to listen. All I heard was my own heart pounding. I went back and checked under Amanda's bed, in her closet, in Mr. and Ms. Ludlows' bedroom, and everywhere else I could think of, but Amanda wasn't there.

Panic smothered me like a blanket. I felt like I couldn't breathe. I could barely think about what to do next. I went downstairs with my dad's words of warning echoing in my head. As I walked down the hallway, I noticed that the front door was opened a little. I flung it open and ran outside.

"Amanda! Where are you?" I yelled. I ran

out to the sidewalk. There was no sign of her in either direction. I didn't know which way to run. Then, suddenly, I remembered the creek behind the house.

I raced to the backyard. Amanda wasn't in her sandbox or on the gym set. I headed for the woods. The slope was so steep that my feet slid out from under me. I twisted my ankle, but I couldn't be concerned with that at that moment.

I stumbled and slid down the slope, grabbing at dead branches to keep from falling. I heard rushing water ahead. I had a sudden terrifying thought that if Amanda had waded into the water, she couldn't survive the current. My fear made me scramble faster. And then I heard her.

Amanda was stooping at the edge of the creek bank talking to herself. I gulped back a scream and made a dive for her. Suddenly, she shrieked as she slipped forward. I grabbed the material of her shirt and hauled her back from the creek's edge.

A moment later, we were both sitting on the bank. I was hugging her and crying. Amanda started crying, too.

"It's okay, Amanda," I said over and over as I stroked her hair. "I'll take care of you. Everything's all right now."

When we were both calmer, I held her away from me. "Amanda!" I said sternly. "Don't you ever come down here without your Mommy or Daddy or me. Do you understand? I mean *never!*"

She nodded, and her lower lip trembled. I couldn't bear to make her cry again. I hugged her tightly and then took her hand, and we went in to eat what was left of the soup.

Amanda's bedtime was becoming a difficult ordeal. Each week, bedtime seemed to get worse. She didn't fight me exactly. She just wouldn't go to bed. One night I even had to read six little books to her before she even closed her eyes. She also cried whenever I turned out the light. At first, she would fall asleep quickly. But after a while, Amanda would scream unless I left the light on all the time. Often, she'd follow me back downstairs, and I'd have to take her back up to bed. I was always exhausted at night.

When I woke up the next morning, my first thought was of Ms. Ludlow. It was Friday, the night of the big high school football game. Our family had made plans to go together. But I was worried, because Ms. Ludlow never seemed to get home by 5:00. She always had an excuse, but I wondered if she even tried.

As I grabbed a quick breakfast of toast and

orange juice, Mom reminded me about the game. "Please try not to be late, Mackenzie. Okay?" Mom asked.

"I'll do my best, Mom," I said. I decided to mention our plans to Ms. Ludlow after class.

But after class Ms. Ludlow was busy showing off her new photo enlargers to some of the other teachers. I didn't feel comfortable about interrupting them.

That afternoon as I watched the clock, I was upset with myself for not talking to Ms. Ludlow about my plans to go to the football game. She was late, as usual. The clock crept steadily past 5:00, and there was no call. Amanda grew restless. I sat her down to color, but she wasn't interested. Then I read to her. After a few minutes, she jumped off the couch and ran to the front window.

I continued to read her book out loud, hoping that she'd sit down again and listen. Instead, she began walking precariously across the couch cushions.

"Amanda, come back here," I said. Amanda came back with one jump, bouncing right over me and landing on the other side of the couch.

"That's enough of that," I said. Then Amanda began jumping up and down. "No, Amanda, you cannot jump on the couch." I picked her up and put her on the floor.

"Cookie!" Amanda demanded as she took off toward the kitchen.

"No, Amanda," I said as I followed her. "Your mother will be home any minute. You can't ruin your supper."

Amanda had already begun pushing the chair toward the counter when I stopped her. Then she started to cry. I tried to distract her with crayons, toys, and games, but Amanda just stood in the kitchen wailing," Cookie! I want cookie!"

I decided that Amanda must really be hungry. I tried to call Ms. Ludlow at school to ask what to do, but there was no answer in the photography room.

I looked in the refrigerator. It was nearly empty. I did find a few carrots in the crisper and quickly peeled and cleaned them for Amanda to eat. I held a carrot out to her, but she slapped it out of my hand and onto the floor.

"Amanda, you stop that now," I said. She started to cry again. Amanda ran across the room. She shoved the swinging door hard as she pushed her way through it. The door swung back and hit her forehead, knocking her down.

"Amanda!" I cried. I dashed after her, afraid she had hurt herself. But she scrambled up and ran through the living room and upstairs. I followed her to the bathroom, but she slammed the door in my face. I assumed she needed to go to the bathroom. I tried to be calm.

I called, "Come down when you're finished, and I'll fix you a snack, Amanda." Then I went downstairs. The next thing I heard was loud, rhythmic bumping from upstairs. I hurried up to find Amanda was still in the bathroom and banging on the door. I could hear her sobs, but when I tried to open the door, the knob wouldn't turn.

"Amanda!" I called. "Amanda, listen to me. Open the door. Open it right now."

"I can't," she said. "Mackie!" Amanda was crying hard. She bumped against the door.

The Ludlows' big, old-fashioned house had those keyholes that take the long keys in every door. I told Amanda to turn the key. She sobbed as she wiggled it, but it didn't unlock. "Mackie!" she cried as she bumped against the door again.

"Amanda! Listen to me." I made a quick check of all the doors in the upstairs. None of them had keys. "Amanda, you must have the key!" I yelled to her through the door.

She was crying hysterically, in great big, hiccuping sobs. "Open door, Mackie!"

I tried to sound calm. "Amanda, just listen to me. Stop crying. You can do this," I said. "Remember what a big girl you are." I tried to talk in my calmest voice, even though I was nearly panicking. "I'll hold the door tightly so the key will turn," I told her. "You lean against it while you turn the key, okay?"

There was a rattle and then a click. "Stop there," I told her. I opened the door, and Amanda fell into my arms crying. I held her close and stroked her hair. Then I told her she was very brave and smart to open the door all by herself.

Then I noticed the brand-new bruise on her forehead. It was right on top of the old one. I realized it came from the bumping. She had been bumping her head against the door.

I hugged her again for just a moment. I felt like I didn't want to let go of her. Then we started for the stairs.

When I stood up, I began trembling all over. My legs felt like they might not make it down the stairs.

"Bad door!" Amanda accused the bathroom.

I felt weak from my neck to my ankles, and I wanted to cry myself. There was something odd and strangely familiar about Amanda's "bad door" comment, but I couldn't place what it was. I took Amanda into the kitchen and put her into her chair at the table. Then I dampened a paper towel and wiped her teary face.

"Let me see if you're hurt," I said.

Amanda was calmer. I examined her bump and saw that it was small. I handed her another piece of carrot. "I don't care what your mother has planned," I said. "I'm getting you something to eat."

I found peanut butter and bread and fixed a sandwich. Amanda finished it and was working on the cookie when Ms. Ludlow walked in just after 6:00.

"Mackenzie, I wish you wouldn't give her cookies," Ms. Ludlow said. "It will ruin her supper."

"She's also had a peanut butter sandwich and a carrot," I said evenly. "I tried to call you, but there wasn't any answer."

"I was in the darkroom and couldn't leave to answer the phone," Ms. Ludlow said shortly. "What did you want? Was something wrong?"

"Amanda was very upset and fussy today. I didn't know whether to get her some supper. I had no idea how late you would be. I called to see when you'd be home. Amanda ran into the kitchen door, and then got locked in the bathroom. She bumped her head on the door. I think she's all right, but she needed something to eat and kept asking for a cookie. When I couldn't reach you, I gave her what I found."

Ms. Ludlow's face turned white. "Well, that was probably good then that you gave her a cookie," she said. "Thank you, Mackenzie."

I looked at the clock on the wall. I wanted to say something about her being late again, but she looked so preoccupied that I decided not to. She'd just get angry. I grabbed my bag and jacket.

"Mackie! Don't go!" Amanda yelled. She grabbed my leg, and I had to pry her hands away to get out the door. Amanda was still crying when I left.

Even though I hurried home just as soon as Ms. Ludlow arrived, my mother gave me a disapproving look when I walked in. "Didn't I ask you to call when you're late?" she asked as soon as I walked in.

I gulped. I knew that I should have called, but I didn't have a chance.

"Mackenzie," Mom said, "you know that we have dinner at 5:30. Bobbie can't wait much longer than that. Besides, you know that tonight's the big game." She shoved a loose strand of her hair from her eyes and frowned. "I've kept your dinner warm in the oven."

I hung my bag on the peg by the back door and followed my mother into the kitchen. "Do you want me to leave Amanda all alone when her mother hasn't come home from work yet?" I demanded.

Mother turned from the stove and brought me a pie tin with servings of dried meatloaf and scalloped potatoes. It all looked a little dry, so I got some ketchup from the refrigerator.

Mom pulled out a chair to sit with me while I ate. "I'd like you to tell Ms. Ludlow that she has to get home on time."

"I will," I promised. "It just wasn't a good time to tell her tonight."

Mother frowned. "Well, you'd better do it soon then."

Eight

"I'LL get it!" I shouted as the telephone rang, just after I finished dinner. I grabbed for the phone in the hallway. "Hello," I said.

"Hi. This is Mike Herrell," a voice on the other end said.

"Oh, hi," I said as a wave of disappointment ran through me. *What if he's calling to cancel our trip to the museum?*

"Uh, I was wondering how the pictures of Amanda turned out," he said.

"You were right. They were pretty crummy. I guess I have a lot to learn about using a camera," I admitted.

"It helps if you get to work with others involved in taking photos, too, like on the yearbook staff. The kids are great and give you a lot of tips, so you don't tend to make the same mistakes all the time."

"That's a good idea. I'll think about it." *But where would I ever find the time to do something like that*? I wondered.

"It's a shame that you can't stay after school," Mike said. "But you're probably going to get rich from all the money you're making at baby-sitting. You'll be able to take a trip around the world or do something wild with all your money."

I laughed. "I'm saving for a camera of my own. I stopped by Main Street Camera the other day, and it looks like I'll be baby-sitting forever before I can afford a neat camera."

Mike laughed. "What about the *Courier's* photo competition?" he asked me. "The top prize is $200."

"Did you enter?" I asked him.

"I won third place last year," he said. "That's how I was able to buy my camera."

"I was hoping to get some pictures of Amanda that I could enter," I said. "But nothing was good enough."

"We could try again," Mike suggested. "What about Sunday afternoon when Amanda isn't so tired? You could probably talk Ms. Ludlow into loaning her to us again."

I felt a spark run through my veins. Mike hadn't called to cancel our date after all. Here he was asking to see me on Sunday, too.

"That would be great," I said.

"Check with Ms. Ludlow to see if it's okay. If it is, then how does Sunday around 2:00 sound?"

"That sounds great."

We hung up after that, but just a minute later, Mike called back.

"I forgot the real reason I called," he said. "Are we still on for the exhibit at the museum tomorrow?"

"Sure!" I was having a hard time keeping the excitement out of my voice.

"Okay. I'll be there at 1:00."

"Do you know where I live?" I asked.

"Oops," Mike said with an embarrassed laugh. "I guess I was waiting to ask you that during my third phone call a minute or two from now."

I laughed. "I'm at 73 Ridgeview."

"I know where that is. You're really close to the Ludlows, right?" he asked.

"Yeah, we're just across the creek," I said.

"Well, I'd better get going. I'm taking pictures tonight at the football game. Are you going to be there?" Mike asked.

"Of course," I said. Twenty minutes ago when I was eating my dried out supper, all I felt like doing was going to my room and sleeping. But suddenly I felt better. I couldn't wait to go to the football game.

"Great!" Mike said. "Maybe I'll see you. You'll be sure to see me. I'll be the one on the sidelines trying not to get run over by the team."

I giggled. We hung up after that, and I remembered I'd never asked Mom if it was all right to go out with Mike. I raced into the living room. "Mom, is it all right if I go to the museum with Mike Herrell tomorrow?"

"Uh-oh!" Alan teased. "Mac's got a date! Now we'll really have to watch out for her. Don't worry, Mom. I'll be glad to go along and chaperon for her."

"Alan Tyler, if you so much as come within three blocks of the museum, I'll—"

"You'll what?" he asked with a big grin.

"I'll take your arm off and hit you over the head with it!" I said.

"Ouch. Oh, my arm, my arm," Alan yelled. Finally, he stopped dancing around the room. "And how are you going to do that?"

"By physical force, if necessary," I said, turning back to Mother. "So, is it okay if I go?"

"Yes, I suppose so. Who is this boy?" she asked.

"Mike Herrell. He's the one I told you about. He's in my photography class, and he works on our school yearbook. He's really good. He even won third prize in the *Courier's* photo contest last year. He's the one who helped me take the photos of Amanda."

"He sounds like a nice young man," Mom said. "But I would like to meet him."

"Can you keep Alan from teasing me, please? I don't want to be embarrassed when he comes over," I said.

Mom nodded. "I'll threaten to go with him on *his* dates." We both hooted with laughter at the thought of Mom on Alan's dates.

"Oh, I better go call Anne. Maybe she'll go to the game with us."

"Good idea," Mom said. "I'm glad to see you doing things with your friends again."

＊　＊　＊　＊　＊

Mom kept her promise. On Saturday morning, she sent Alan off on a few errands to get him out of my way. I decided to wear my favorite jeans. Then I changed into a skirt, and finally back into my jeans.

What would Anne wear? I wondered. I picked up my skirt again as I thought about the evening before. Anne had been surprised when I told her about my date. She really enjoyed saying, "I told you so."

Suddenly, the phone rang, interrupting my thoughts.

"It's for you, Mackenzie," my mom called.

I hoped it wasn't Mike canceling out, I thought, as I picked up the receiver. I was surprised that it was Ms. Ludlow.

"Mackenzie? Hi. Dan and I would like to visit a camera exhibit this afternoon. I wondered if you could watch Amanda for us."

"Oh, Ms. Ludlow. I'd like to but I can't. I'm going to the exhibit, too."

"Oh. Well, maybe we'll just skip it then," she said. Her voice dropped in disappointment.

I hoped that by turning her down I wouldn't lose my job. I really didn't know why she couldn't take Amanda along for one day.

"Maybe I could call you when I get back," I offered. I really didn't want to hurry back from my date, but I felt so guilty for keeping her from going. I could hear my mom's voice telling me that I deserved some free time, too. But I easily pushed that thought to the back of my mind.

"That's very nice of you, Mackenzie. Yes, please call," Ms. Ludlow said. "Amanda likes you so much, and I appreciate you staying with her."

Mike arrived a few minutes later and, after

I introduced him to mom, we walked the four blocks downtown to the museum. On the way, he told me that he hadn't really had any hobbies until last year when Ms. Ludlow introduced him to photography.

"But you're already the photographer for the yearbook," I said. "And you photographed the game..."

"Yes, but that's because I learned a lot last year," Mike said. "After I got started, I loved working and experimenting with film and lighting. It's like trying to catch a moment and make it stand still. Sometimes it doesn't work, but when it does..."

"You really like Ms. Ludlow, don't you?" I asked him.

"Doesn't everybody?" he asked. "Yes, she is special to me. Last year, my parents split up and she was there to talk with me a lot. By showing me her love of photography, it kind of gave me a purpose, too. And she introduced me to a counselor, who really helped me." He paused. "That was a bad time, and she was a real friend. I appreciate that."

I realized that Mike probably didn't share these feelings with very many people. I was happy that he was telling me. Suddenly, he must have felt self-conscious, because he laughed and started joking around again.

The exhibit was fascinating. But I admit that Mike might have been part of the reason. We stopped at every display, while Mike explained the old cameras to me and told stories of early-day photographers.

"Watch this," Mike said as we stopped at something that looked like a round black lampshade.

"What do I watch?" I asked.

"Just peek through these slots as I spin it," he instructed. He sent the lampshade whirling while I stared at its side. As the slits in the side came past me, I saw a continuous picture of horses jumping over a fence.

"How did you get to know so much about cameras?" I asked him.

He shrugged. "I guess I read a book or something."

"Or maybe 10 books?"

Mike looked away. "Let's look at the old card-flippers from an arcade," he suggested.

We peeked through the eyepieces of the old iron machines and turned the cranks. Pictures flipped in succession to give the illusion of moving. "It's like when you draw a different picture on the corner of the page of a tablet and flip through the pages," I said.

"And that's how movies are made," Mike said with a smile. "But the reel does the flipping more evenly than a person can."

"Mike, that was a great exhibit," I told him as we walked outside into the sunshine. "I'd never have gone through if you hadn't suggested it."

"Are you thirsty after all that history?" Mike asked. "How about stopping off at Nicole's Ice Cream Shoppe?"

I opened my mouth to say yes, but then I remembered Amanda. "Oh, I'm sorry, but I'd better get home. I have another commitment."

He gave me a puzzled look, but he didn't ask me what it was. As we walked along, a cloud of silence seemed to expand between us. I began to feel uncomfortable.

"Uh, Mike, Ms. Ludlow wanted to see the exhibit, too. So I told her that I'd watch Amanda so she could go with her husband."

"You sure stay with Amanda a lot, don't you?"

"Yes, I guess I do," I admitted. "Sometimes I wish..."

I didn't finish what I was saying, because I didn't have an answer. I didn't mind caring for Amanda, but I just wished that Ms. Ludlow was more reliable. When we got to my front door, Mike didn't mention anything about taking pictures at the park on Sunday.

I tried to force myself to stop thinking about

Mike. I didn't have time. I had to get over to Ms. Ludlow's house. I went into the kitchen and quickly dialed her number. The line was busy.

My mom came into the kitchen then. "How was your day?" she asked me. "Did you have a good time?"

"Yes, I really did. I learned a lot about photography today."

"You're home early, aren't you?" Mom asked.

"Yeah, I have some other things I need to do. Besides, we're going to the park to photograph Amanda tomorrow. Anyway, I told Ms. Ludlow that I'd look after Amanda for a little while today so she could see the exhibit, too."

Mom looked at me funny, but she didn't say anything. I hurried to the hall phone and dialed Ms. Ludlow's again. It was still busy.

Mom came through the hallway as I put down the phone.

"Nobody there?" she asked.

"Just busy," I said.

"Well, I want to talk with you, Mackenzie." I followed her into the kitchen, and we sat down at the table. Mom tilted her head and stared at me with concern in her eyes. "Mac, I think you're too involved with Amanda."

"No, I'm not, Mom," I said defensively. "I just baby-sit her. That's all."

Mom shook her head. "When you come home early from your first real date just to baby-sit a four-year-old girl, you are becoming too involved."

"It's not like that," I tried to explain. "But Ms. Ludlow asked me, and she is my photography teacher. She should see the exhibit, too."

"Why can't Amanda go with her parents to the exhibit?" Mom asked.

"Well, she's very active and hard to handle sometimes. But there is something that worries me. Amanda has these bruises, and she's always scared of going to bed."

Mom frowned. "That may be normal. Little kids do get bruised a lot, especially active ones. But I think that maybe you should talk with your school counselor about this. She might be able to tell you whether there's something to worry about."

I thought about it for a moment. "But if there's nothing really wrong, I'd feel terrible. I mean, Ms. Ludlow is my teacher."

"That's a good point."

"But Mike mentioned that he talked with a counselor. Maybe I could ask him who it was," I said.

"It sounds like a good idea," Mom agreed.

I waited a few more minutes, then tried Ms. Ludlow's number again. It was still busy. I finally grabbed my coat and walked over to their house.

As I walked, I thought about my first date. It was weird that I thought Mike was a snob when I first met him. Today, he seemed so much the opposite. His eyes lit up whenever he talked about interesting photos that he'd taken. I realized that he was shy and definitely not a snob.

When I reached the Ludlow house, I had to knock three times before someone answered. The girl who came to the door looked about 10 years old.

"Yeah?" she asked. "What do you want?"

I looked into her pale, frightened eyes.

"Um, excuse me. Is this the Ludlow house?" I asked.

The girl shook her head yes. "I'm the baby-sitter."

"Oh," I said. I couldn't believe that Ms. Ludlow would allow Amanda to be here with this 10 year old. "I'll come back later."

I started to leave, but I heard Amanda yell, "Mackie! Mackie!"

"Hi, Amanda."

"She's playing with her stuffed animals. I

89

can't let you in," the sitter said.

"That's fine," I told her. "I'll see you later, Amanda."

"Mackie! Don't go!" Amanda wailed. She burst into tears.

I was getting used to Amanda's outbursts. "It's all right. I'll be back later." I turned to the sitter. She looked at Amanda like she had no idea what to do with her. "I sit for her a lot of the time. She'll be okay again after I leave."

"Don't go, Mackie!" Amanda wailed.

"Just close the door," I told the sitter.

She looked down at Amanda and said, "Come on, please don't cry."

Then Amanda pounded on the door with her fists and her head. The sitter looked frightened. "Stop that, Amanda. Right now," I said.

She stopped. "You be good now," I said and walked down the sidewalk.

"Mr. and Mrs. Ludlow should be back about 7:00," the sitter called after me. "Try them then."

I nodded without turning around. Amanda started to yell again. I called over my shoulder. "It's okay, Amanda. Get back from the door."

The door closed, but I could still hear

Amanda's muffled cries. All the way home, I grumbled at myself for being a fool. I shouldn't have gone over there. It wasn't my business.

As I walked in the cold sunlight, I tried to remember the great time I'd had earlier with Mike. I was sorry now that I had come home so soon from our date. I guess the Ludlows didn't need me to baby-sit after all. I wasn't as important to them as I thought I was. But all evening I couldn't get the scene with Amanda and the young baby-sitter out of my mind.

Nine

IT'S terrible when somebody you really like turns out to be different than you thought. No, I don't mean Mike—we had a great time together Sunday! When we went over to pick up Amanda, we met Ms. Ludlow's husband.

Then we went to the park and took lots of great pictures of Amanda. We fed the ducks again, and Mike helped her climb into a little tree. I took a shot of her sitting on a limb with the leafless branches crisscrossing the gray sky behind her.

It was Mike's idea to try that picture just that way. To get the angle that I needed, I had to lie flat on my back in the grass.

"I'm probably crawling with bugs," I grumbled as I stood up and brushed off my jeans.

"Yeah, but it'll be worth it," Mike said. He lifted Amanda out of the tree and set her down to the ground.

She dashed across the field yelling, "Swing me, Mike!" But Mike stood staring at me. He picked a leaf out of my hair. There was a funny look on his face. I thought he might touch my hair again. But the next moment, he said, "What's green with nine little segments and 18 legs?"

I said, "I don't know."

He said, "I don't know either, but it's crawling across your ear."

I grabbed for my ear before I realized that he was teasing, and then I yelled, "Oh, Mike Herrell! I'll get you for that!"

But he was already running across the field right behind Amanda. His shouts of laughter drifted back to me.

After we dropped Amanda off at her house, I got up the courage to ask him about the counselor he went to. Right away, he became serious. "Is something wrong, Mackenzie?"

I shook my head. "No, at least, I don't think so. I just keep thinking about some of the stuff Amanda does. She gets so scared to go to bed, and..." I shrugged my shoulders. "It's probably nothing, but—"

"I'll call her," Mike interrupted me. "You can probably stop by to see her tomorrow. Don't worry. It will be fine."

Mike even met me at the counselor's office after I left Amanda on Monday. The office door opened, and a woman about my height came out to greet us. She had sandy-colored hair, brown eyes, and a smile that widened when she said hello to Mike.

"Mac, this is Mrs. Caris," he introduced us. "Mrs. Caris, this is Mackenzie Tyler."

Mrs. Caris smiled at me.

"Mackenzie, Mike is one of my favorite people. I'm glad to know any of his friends. Come in, and tell me how I can help you." She led me toward her office, and Mike left, saying he'd call me later.

Mrs. Caris had a comfortable office with a beatiful wooden desk and a couple of cozy chairs. There were some pretty pictures of flowers on the wall. I don't know what I expected, but I felt comfortable with her right away. I told her that I didn't know if there was a problem or not. Then I told her about Amanda.

"Do you think she's being abused?" Mrs. Caris asked me.

"Oh, no!" I said firmly. "Ms. Ludlow isn't like that at all. She's so nice to the kids at school, and she's really helpful to everyone. I know that Amanda gave herself at least one of the bruises. She locked herself in the bath-

94

room, and when she couldn't get out, she really panicked. She was beating her head against the door trying to get out." I thought a minute. "I'm sure she probably causes her own injuries. I really don't know why I came here. It's just that there's something—I don't know."

"When people are trying to be parents and have a job at the same time, they may have to struggle a bit to adjust their priorities," Mrs. Caris said. "You do seem to baby-sit for the little girl a great deal."

"But I really like to do it," I said. "I don't mind, really I don't."

"Well, if you ever do mind, or if anything else occurs, please feel free to call me anytime," Mrs. Caris said. She wrote on a card and handed it to me. "If I'm not here, I've written my home number there, too."

It was odd—Mrs. Caris didn't give me any advice, but I felt better, anyway. I was glad Mike had introduced us.

Anne always tells me that I have an active imagination. She says I can smell danger miles away when it's not real. Every time we sat over our lunches together in the cafeteria, she asked me about Ms. Ludlow and Amanda. When I tried to tell her about Amanda's getting banged up, Anne's reply was that

Amanda was so bright and curious.

"She probably gets it from her mother," Anne said. Her eyes followed Ms. Ludlow across the lunchroom. "She has perfect style. She always has time to talk to people. She's what my grandmother would call a gracious lady."

I started to tell Anne that Ms. Ludlow wasn't exactly like that, but she wouldn't listen to me.

"Mac, I don't know what would satisfy you. You've got a terrific job, and you get to have everyday contact with the greatest teacher at Brighton—probably in all of Brookview. And all you do is complain.

I didn't say anything. I couldn't. It wouldn't matter, anyway. Besides, from Anne's point of view, she was right. Ms. Ludlow was terrific as a teacher. She showed us how to develop film. She guided us through portraits, and showed us how to enlarge them on the new equipment. She let us practice printing some of the pictures she was doing for the astronomy book. During my study hall on Thursday, she even helped me pick out the photo to enter in the *Courier*'s contest and helped me get it out in the mail.

"It's a great shot, Mackenzie. You did a wonderful job with it," Ms. Ludlow said. I picked the photo of Amanda in the tree. Getting grass in my hair had been worth it after all.

* * * * *

On Thursday night, I missed Alan's big varsity quiz team meet because I was baby-sitting for Amanda. His team was in the finals for the championship. It seemed like ages ago that I'd promised him I wouldn't miss that meet no matter what. But when the day came, I could only promise to think of him that evening.

I didn't do much thinking of him either, because Amanda kept me too busy.

I vowed I'd get Amanda to bed early because I had to watch a television special on the vanishing wetlands for my science class. By the time she played in the tub for a while and then had me read three books to her, it was almost time for the show.

"That's enough, Amanda," I told her as I put down the last book. "Now you crawl into bed." I gave her a kiss, and tucked her in.

But when I started to leave, she yelled, "No! Don't go, Mackie!"

"Amanda, it's time to go to sleep. I'll be right downstairs," I said. "I'm not going anywhere." I reached for the doorknob.

"No!" she cried loudly. "No door. Leave it open!"

"Okay, okay," I said. "I'll leave it wide open, but don't let the TV keep you awake. I have to watch a special show."

"I go asleep. Promise. Leave the door open." She slid down under her blanket to demonstrate that she was willing to sleep.

I hurried downstairs and turned on the television. "Mackie!" Amanda called.

"What?" I called up the stairs.

"Can I have a drink?" she asked.

The commercials were still on. I scurried up and gave Amanda a drink. Then I ran down and sat on the floor in front of the TV so that I could keep the volume low.

"Mackie!" Amanda called. I ignored her. But she called again. "Mackie! Mackie! Mackie!"

"Go to sleep, Amanda!" I yelled up to her.

"I'm cold!" she yelled.

"Pull up another blanket!" I yelled back.

"Mackie!"

I went to the foot of the stairs and called up to her, "Amanda, if you want your door left open, you be quiet right now. Otherwise, I'll close that door."

That gave me silence for all of 15 minutes. I picked up my pad of paper to make some notes on the show. The next thing I knew, Amanda came downstairs carrying her favorite bear, Louie, and dragging a blanket behind her. She plopped on the floor beside me and spread her blanket over our legs.

"Amanda," I said. I was feeling exasperated, but I didn't want to miss the show. It was pretty good even if it was an assignment. Amanda curled up and leaned against me. I spread the blanket over her and held my arm around her. So much for taking notes.

"You can't talk," I told her. "I have to watch this for school."

She nodded and closed her eyes. But the next minute, the TV was showing large flocks of wild ducks. Amanda sat up. "Is that—" Before she had a chance to start asking questions, I shushed her. "I'll tell you later, okay, Amanda?"

She was pretty quiet after that, but at the commercial she asked me about the ducks. "Why are duckies dying?" she wanted to know.

I didn't know if Amanda knew what dying meant, so I said, "Well, they don't have anyplace to live or get food."

"No dinner?" she wanted to know.

"Well, no," I said. "They're hungry, and there isn't enough food. And there's no place to live because their land is being taken away."

I paused a moment before I said, "All right, young lady. You get to bed now."

We went upstairs, and this time she fell asleep almost as soon as she got into bed.

Ms. Ludlow took me home when she arrived. I told her that I would walk, but she insisted. She went up to check on Amanda and then hurried me home. Again I wondered how smart it was to leave Amanda alone—even for just a few minutes. And I wondered how often she did it.

The next morning at breakfast, Mom reminded me again about being late.

"Mackenzie, now don't be late tonight," she said. "Remember that we're going out to celebrate with the varsity quiz team and their families. Be sure to tell Ms. Ludlow you have to get home on time tonight."

"I will. I promise," I said as I gulped my milk and scrambled to get my books together for school. Alan had left already. He was so excited about winning that scholarship last night that he was actually the first one out of bed in the morning. I was really proud of him, and my parents were about to burst. My dad could hardly stop grinning.

I did tell Ms. Ludlow that I had to be home at 5:00 that night. I even told her the reason.

"Of course, Mackenzie. I'll hurry," she said

smiling. "And don't forget to congratulate your brother for me."

I hurried Amanda home without stopping at the park because I knew that Ms. Ludlow would be on time for once. So when it got to be 5:00, and then 5:30, I was afraid that something had happened to Ms. Ludlow. Maybe she had been in an accident. I called the school, but there was no answer. I kept expecting my mother to call any minute, but she didn't.

Amanda was on edge, probably because I was upset. She ran through the house, scattering toys everywhere, and when I tried to get her to help pick them up, she only threw them around the room. I tried to give her a snack, but she refused. Instead, she ran to the front door and tried to pull it open.

"No, Amanda," I said. "We're staying in today."

"I want to go walk! I want to go to the park!" Amanda yelled at me. "You promised!" She banged her fists and her head against the door until I took her hand and led her to the kitchen.

"Well, I can't Amanda," I said sternly. "Not today. I'll take you next week, and that's that."

I know that part of the problem was me. I had no patience with Amanda today. I just wanted to go home.

By the time Ms. Ludlow walked in at 6:30 with a big smile on her face, I was furious.

"Where have you been?" I stormed at her. Any other time I would never have been so rude. Immediately, I clamped my mouth shut and felt guilty.

Ms. Ludlow clapped her hand over her mouth. "Oh, Mackenzie! I'm so sorry. I completely forgot you needed to go home early. I stopped to turn in my photos at the college. While I was there, Dr. Wilson's editor stopped in. I got a chance to show him my portfolio. He talked about the kinds of pictures they want regularly. He wants me to bring my photos and visit their photo editor next week. We got to talking, and I didn't realize how late it was."

I couldn't bring myself to be polite and say, "That's all right." Instead, I just said, "Well, I'd better hurry."

I ran all the way home, even though I knew I was too late. The house was empty. There was a note on the table telling me to fix a hot dog for myself. I didn't bother. I sat down at the kitchen table.

"Maybe Ms. Ludlow's not so perfect after all," I said to the silent kitchen. I could just see all the kids and their families, Alan and

Bobbie and my parents all eating out at a nice restaurant together. I could just see them laughing and joking and talking about their winning meet.

I felt all alone. I thought about all the good times I was missing because I was busy with Amanda. I loved Amanda, but she wasn't enough to make up for losing all my friends. I thought about how I missed getting together with Anne, and how I missed our great after-school talks. I looked at the note again and listened to the empty creaking of our house. I wanted to cry.

After a while, I got up and turned on the TV. I don't remember what I watched, because I don't think I paid any attention to it.

It was after 10:00 when the telephone rang. I figured it was my mother calling to check on me. But the voice on the other end was barely recognizable.

"Mackenzie! Have you seen Amanda?" Ms. Ludlow's voice was shaking. "I mean, she's gone," Ms. Ludlow was sobbing.

I practically dropped the telephone. My heart was pounding fast. "Stay there," I told Ms. Ludlow. "I'll be right over."

Ten

I left a note for my parents, and then I called Anne and Mike and told them to meet me at Ms. Ludlow's.

I ran all the way over to Ms. Ludlow's. My feet pounded on the sidewalk, and my heart pounded in my ears. The cold, full moon stared down on me. How could this have happened?

I burst into the house without knocking. The door was open. Ms. Ludlow sat hunched over in the rocking chair. She was staring blankly ahead of her and rhythmically tearing a tissue into shreds in her lap. All of Amanda's toys were strewn around the way they were when I had left.

"What happened?" I asked.

Tears rolled down Ms. Ludlow's cheeks, smearing her mascara. She shook her head. "Oh, Mackenzie! I don't know," she said. "I just ran down to the school to check my time exposures. I wasn't gone long, maybe 15 minutes or half an hour." She wiped her eyes with what was left of the tissue.

"Did you call the police?" I asked.

Ms. Ludlow looked up, startled. "No! I didn't think of it. Do you suppose—" she gulped. "Somebody took her? Oh, no!" she burst into tears again. Then she looked up at me and said, "She was asleep! And I locked— I locked—I always lock her door. She couldn't have..."

Strangely, everything seemed to be falling into place in my mind. Amanda's bruises and the bumping of her head against the door now made sense. This was not the first time that Ms. Ludlow had left Amanda alone at night. But it was the first time since Amanda had learned—since I taught her—how to unlock a door. I shivered. Then the doorbell rang.

Both Anne and Mike were on the step. I let them in and told them as briefly as possible that Amanda had either been kidnapped or had gotten out on her own.

"I think she's out on her own," I said. "She got out one day when I was here, and I found her out back in the woods. If we split up, we can probably find her right away."

Ms. Ludlow stood up and brushed away her

tears. "I'll find the flashlights," she said, "and call the police."

She paused, and then she said, "That creek is almost a river from the rains. Please find her. Find her before she gets to the creek!"

We hurried. While Ms. Ludlow stayed to talk with the police, Anne, Mike, and I took flashlights and started walking through the little woods toward the creek.

The bright moon made everything stark and ghostly. It's hard enough for me to go through that woods in the daytime. At night, it was like a nightmare. We crossed and crisscrossed through the trees and the prickly underbrush between the house and the creek, calling and calling for Amanda. But somehow I wasn't surprised that there was no answer.

After a while, we saw the flashing lights of the police car reflected in the sky over the house. Then an officer joined us. He took Mike, and they went along the edge of the creek looking for signs of Amanda. I was terrified of what they might find.

Anne was pretty quiet. Finally, she said, "How could she just leave her alone? And I always thought she was so perfect."

I was upset myself. But without thinking, I said, "Maybe she didn't feel like she had any choice. Maybe she needed that job too much to not go after it."

Anne shook her head. Then she said, "What if Amanda walked down the street?"

"Let's go in and see what places are being checked," I said.

"The police are cruising the streets," Ms. Ludlow said to us as we came in. She poured some coffee into a fat mug and held it with trembling hands. "Do you want something to warm you up?"

We shook our heads. The door opened behind her, and Mike came in. He looked at me and shook his head soberly. The room seemed to stand out in sharp relief, but the voices pulled away from me, becoming more and more distant. I saw the teddy bear on the floor, the refrigerator and stove, the littered counter with its assortment of glasses, plates, the open bread bag. I stared at the bag curiously. There was something important about it.

"Mackenzie, are you all right?" Mike's voice seemed to come from far away. Then I felt his hand on my arm.

Anne grabbed my other arm. I heard Anne say, "Quick, she's fainting! Find her a chair."

They pushed me into a kitchen chair, and suddenly I was all right. "I—I'm fine," I said as somebody handed me a glass of water.

Then I looked up at Mike. "I think I know where Amanda is," I said. "It's the bread. The bread is open." He looked at me and grinned.

We all scrambled into a police car and headed for the park. Mike, Anne, and I jumped out the second the car stopped and ran toward the pond.

"We saw this show," I gasped. "Last night. She asked me about the ducks. I told her they were starving."

"Oh, Mackenzie. It's okay," Mike said shortly. "Let's just find her."

We raced to the spot between the trees where we'd always taken her. Mike shined his flashlight all around the area. But she wasn't there.

"Oh, no," Ms. Ludlow wailed as the flashlight beams played over the pond. "She's not—"

I shook my head. "I don't think she fell in," I said. "But this is where we always took her."

"Come on, Mackenzie. Let's walk around the pond," Mike said. "Maybe when she couldn't find them, she went looking."

We skirted the edge of the pond, playing our lights on the water, on the bushes, on the trees and grass near the water. I stopped at every bush, shoving it aside and peering into the clumps of dense brush.

We were on the far side of the pond from everyone else, when I saw a flash of white. "There!" I cried. "By that tree."

Mike turned his flashlight just as I saw her face. She was asleep under the tree, almost completely hidden by a bush. Her fingers were clutched tightly around a wad of mangled bread.

The lights woke her, and she started to cry. I raced to her and picked her up. By the time the others arrived, I was sitting in the wet grass rocking her in my arms and crying.

"Mackie?" she asked sleepily. "Mackie? The ducks gone. They went away."

"No they didn't, Amanda," I told her. "It'll be all right. They'll be back tomorrow. Shh! Shh! Don't cry. I promise, I'll bring you to see them. They're just in bed."

"Went nighty night?" she asked me.

"Yes, Amanda. They're fine. Everything is just fine," I said, even though tears were streaming down my face and my jeans were soaked from sitting in the wet grass.

Ms. Ludlow carried Amanda back to the car. I couldn't seem to stop crying. Mike put his arm around my shoulders and hugged me. Ms. Ludlow thanked us over and over again. Then she got out and took Amanda into the house. The police took Mike, Anne, and me home. As we pulled up to my door, Anne said, "Mackenzie, I know I acted dumb, defending Ms. Ludlow all the time. When you tried to tell me about things that were happening, I didn't understand. I want you to know that I'm sorry."

I nodded. As I got up to leave, I realized I was clutching Mike's hand. I realized it when he gave my hand a little squeeze before he let it go.

Eleven

DAD'S car was in the driveway when I got home. When I got out of the police car, Mike followed me. "I'll get out here," he said quickly. "If your parents are home, I'll stop in just for a minute."

Anne looked at Mike and me, and then she said, "If you're okay, we'll talk tomorrow."

I don't think the police officer was too happy about letting Mike out at my house, but I said, "My parents will take him home." In the kitchen, Mom was packing Bobbie's lunch for the next day. Without looking up, she said, "Mackenzie, you've got to write better notes. I thought you wrote that you were at the Ludlows', but when I called, there was no answer."

She turned around and stared at me—and at Mike. She frowned. "Just where have you been—" she started. Then she saw my face

111

and stopped. "What happened?" she asked.

I sank onto a kitchen chair. Mike answered for me in short, fast sentences. "Amanda disappeared. We found her in the park. The police just brought us back."

"Oh, no!" Mother crossed the room and sat down. She motioned to Mike. He sat down on the chair next to me. "Is she—"

"She's fine," Mike said.

I looked down at my wet jeans. My mind was spinning with the memories of all the things I'd done wrong. I shook my head. "Amanda wanted to go to the park today. She was so upset by a TV show I let her watch that she thought the ducks were dying."

"Mackenzie, it's not your fault," Mike said quietly.

"Why would it be?" Mother wanted to know.

"I'm the one who taught her to open doors," I said. The tears were slipping from my eyes again, and I couldn't stop them. "When she locked herself in the bathroom, I—"

Mike shook his head. "That's not the point, Mac."

"And then tonight, I was in such a hurry to get home for the party—"

"You didn't leave her alone, did you?" Mom asked seriously.

I looked up at mom and Mike. Mike said,

"No, but Ms. Ludlow did."

"I could have stayed. I could have gone back when I realized you'd already left," I started.

Then Mike interrupted me quietly, but very firmly. "Mackenzie, you can't blame yourself. You've got to pull yourself back from this situation. It is not your fault that Ms. Ludlow went out to check her time exposures and left her child alone. There is also nothing wrong with teaching a child to help herself when she locks the bathroom door."

I looked over toward my mother. She nodded her head in agreement.

I turned toward Mike and noticed again his deep and serious eyes. After a long pause, he said, "But there is something wrong with your trying to be Amanda's mother."

My mother stood up. "That's what I've been trying to tell her," she said. "Listen to this young man, Mackenzie. I'll take you home when you want to go, Mike," she said, and then she left the room. I couldn't believe it. Mom felt I was responsible enough to be left to talk to Mike alone.

Mike smiled. "You've been giving all your time to that little girl," he said. "You've been missing out on school activities and friends. You can't make up for Amanda's mother. And you can't take the blame for things when she doesn't act like a mother."

I nodded. I knew he was right. "I thought she was so perfect," I said. I heard a bitterness in my voice that I didn't know was there. "Anne was so sure that she was. And then you said—said—" I couldn't go on.

"I know," Mike agreed. "It never occurred to me that she'd do that. She was good to me when I really needed a friend. But I don't think she's perfect." Mike cocked his head and his mouth turned up in a half-smile. "You can't idolize people, Mackenzie. I learned that last year. I think I know how you're feeling, because that's the way I felt about my dad."

He stopped talking. I looked at him and we were both silent for a while. Then he said very quietly, "When my parents broke up, I couldn't believe it could happen. I found out then that my dad is just like anybody else. He's got strengths and weaknesses, good points and bad ones. Mrs. Caris helped me see that I could still love him even though he wasn't perfect."

Right then I wanted to cry for Mike and for all the hurt he must have felt. But he smiled and shrugged, and then I was grateful that he'd told me. "I wanted to be just like her," I said angrily.

"It'll be all right, Mac. Give yourself and

Ms. Ludlow a chance," he said. He squeezed my hand, and I tried to smile back at him, even though I wasn't sure I could ever give her another chance. Something in the way Mike looked at me made me think of something else, though. For the first time this awful evening, I realized I must look a mess.

"So, Mackenzie, what're you going to do about this situation?" he asked me.

I shook my head. "I don't know."

"Well, will you promise to think about pulling yourself back from so much babysitting?" he asked.

I nodded, and he stood up. "And did you say I could have a ride home?"

I grinned. As we walked into the living room, I said, "Mike, I'm glad you're my friend."

"Me, too," he said.

That wasn't the end of that night's conversations. After we took Mike home, I stayed up talking with Mom and Dad. "You've got to talk with Ms. Ludlow, Mac," Dad said. "It's against the law to leave a child alone. If she continues to do that, we'll have to call the authorities."

"Oh, Dad, I don't think she'd do it again," I said. But my stomach turned over at the thought of talking with her, anyway.

"You liked that counselor," Mother observed. "Maybe you could suggest her to Ms. Ludlow."

I worried all the next day about talking with Ms. Ludlow. And I wondered how I'd get to talk with her when she always had a ton of kids gathering around with questions. But she asked me to stay after class, and I waited until the other kids cleared out.

Ms. Ludlow wore that beautiful green dress, but her makeup couldn't hide the dark circles under her eyes. I probably looked just as bad. When I went up to her desk, she smiled brightly and said, "Mackenzie, I wanted to thank you for all your help last night."

I hung my head. "Sure," I said. Then I gulped while I tried to gather some courage. "Uh—Ms. Ludlow. Can—can we talk?"

"Of course," Ms. Ludlow smiled that wonderful smile that the kids love. But to me it just looked phony.

"Uh—that is—" I started. Then it all came tumbling out in a rush. "Ms. Ludlow, I can't stay with Amanda every day. I'm missing all my photo lab time, and my parents said I need more time for myself. And also, you can't leave Amanda alone anymore. She knows how to open doors because I taught her. Besides she wakes up and bumps against the door. That's where all the bruises come from. And—and it's too dangerous. And it's against the law."

Ms. Ludlow's lip quivered, but she clamped it tightly shut.

"That will be enough, Mackenzie," Ms. Ludlow said sharply. "I believe that is enough interfering from you. If you don't wish to baby-sit for Amanda, I'm sure I can find someone else."

"But that's not what I want!" I protested. "I love Amanda. I love to baby-sit for her!" For a minute I almost wanted to say I'd come over anytime, day or night, just so Amanda wouldn't be alone. I wanted to say it. But then I remembered all the things Mike told me, and I stepped back.

Ms. Ludlow's eyes were cold. "I shall make other arrangements," she said. "Perhaps you could pick her up today, though, since your decision has given me no notice."

I nodded. I couldn't talk because I was just about ready to cry again. I didn't know what to do, so I turned and went to my next class.

All afternoon I could hardly figure out what was going on in my classes. I felt like I'd swallowed a barbed wire fence and now it was tearing my insides apart. It was awful to see Ms. Ludlow so angry with me. I'd been so crazy about her. Losing a friend is the most painful thing. The soreness in my heart was like a deep dry well that went down and down with no bottom. And then I was scared about Amanda. Who would take care of her? What if Ms. Ludlow left her alone again?

I was buttoning Amanda's coat at the Kid Connection when Ms. Ludlow walked in. For a moment, we stood and stared at each other. I didn't know what to say.

But Amanda did. "Mommy!" she yelled as she raced across the room and threw herself into Ms. Ludlow's legs.

"Hi, there, honey," Ms. Ludlow said as she smiled and stroked Amanda's hair. Then she looked up at me, "How about if we take a walk?" she asked.

I nodded. Amanda was decisive. "Go to the park. We'll feed the ducks," she said. "Ducks are hungry. No dinner."

But Ms. Ludlow said, "Of course, we'll feed them, Amanda. I've got a whole loaf of bread."

We walked through the park together. Ms. Ludlow stopped to push Amanda on the swing for a while. She and Amanda were laughing together and having a great time. I thought how beautiful they looked together and realized I'd never seen Ms. Ludlow play with Amanda before. Then Amanda took off toward the pond. "Let's feed the ducks!" she shouted.

"Here, ducks! Here, ducks!"

I started after her, but Ms. Ludlow came up beside me and said, "We can walk. She's not going that fast."

I slowed down, and after a moment, Ms. Ludlow said, "You were right, Mackenzie. You made me think today."

"I didn't mean—"

"Yes, you did," she interrupted. "And you were right." She paused. I watched Amanda's head bobbing in the meadow ahead of us. She stopped to look at a leaf on the ground. Ms. Ludlow went on. "I realized I've been too busy. When Dan got transferred, I guess I figured I had to do everything at once. We wanted to have extra money to fix up the house. And then I started the photo lab and wanted to get everything going right away. Then my course at the college came along. I've wanted to start my own studio for a long time. Then when I got that offer to do the textbook photos—" She stopped.

When we reached the pond, we stopped walking. Amanda stood on the bank and called, "Ducks! Come here, ducks!" Ms. Ludlow opened the bread and handed several small pieces to Amanda. At first there was no sign of them, but then they came from behind a floating log and sailed across the water toward us—all six of them.

Ms. Ludlow said, "I got so caught up in all those things that I forgot to pay attention to the important ones. Then last night after we were so scared. And today, when you told me you didn't want to baby-sit, I guess I was angry that it messed up my organized schedule," she said. "It sounds awfully silly, doesn't it?"

"No, it doesn't," I said. I was thinking that Ms. Ludlow's schedule was busier than mine. And sometimes I was angry when my schedule got messed up—like I got angry when Ms. Ludlow came home late.

"After today when you said those things, I realized two things," Ms. Ludlow said. "First, I'm trying to do too many things at once. I've got to learn to pull back from some of them and set up priorities." She sat down and plucked a still-green blade of grass and then held it up to the light and studied it intently. "The other thing was that I realized I was forcing the same impossible schedule on you, Mackenzie. And for that, I'm sorry."

"It's okay," I started, but she held up her hand.

"No, it's not," Ms. Ludlow said. "I should never have asked you to take on so much of Amanda's time. You're too young to be a full-time substitute mother. Besides, I was getting too jealous of you."

"Of me?" I asked. That seemed incredible to me.

"Sure," she said. "You were getting to play with Amanda while I only had time for work." She straightened her shoulders. "Well, it's got to stop," she said decisively.

I looked at the firm line drawn on her lips even as she helped Amanda toss bread to the ducks. "What'll you do?" I asked.

"Well, to start with," she said, "I asked Mrs. Goodman about letting Amanda stay later a couple nights a week. She said the center has had a lot of requests for later hours, and they're going to start it on a trial basis. The other days I'm going home with Amanda."

She turned to me. "Mackenzie, I appreciate all the work you've done, and I know you love Amanda. You will always be welcome to come and play with her or take her to the park, but I'll take care of the after-school times. I'd still be happy if you'd sit for me on Thursday evenings until classes end this term."

I nodded. I still thought Ms. Ludlow might need some help figuring out what to do. I wondered whether to suggest a counselor like Mrs. Caris.

But she said, "I know a family counselor. Maybe I'll give her a call. After you spoke to me today, I kept thinking that I could use some help figuring out what's important and what's not."

"Mike said you introduced him to Mrs. Caris," I said carefully. "He said she was terrific."

Ms. Ludlow nodded. "You'd think I'd be smart enough to know when I'm too involved in too many things, wouldn't you, Mackenzie?" She shook her head. "They just crept up on me."

All the time Ms. Ludlow talked, and even afterward as I walked home, I thought about all the things she said. Ms. Ludlow's words sounded a lot like some I'd heard from Mom, Dad, Anne, and Mike—except they were talking about me. Maybe part of the reason I had idolized Ms. Ludlow was that I was a lot like her.

I decided that whether I bought a new camera or not, I was just as happy to be able to come home after school. For a minute, I thought that would give me a chance to work in the photo lab, and perhaps join the yearbook or the newspaper staff. Then I caught myself just in time.

"Try one thing, Mackenzie, not all of them," I told myself.

Twelve

"THIS is a nice party," I said.

"It sure is," Mike agreed. He picked up his spoon to attack his sundae, but at the last minute he grabbed the cherry off of mine.

"No fair!" I protested, but I couldn't even make myself pretend to be angry. I looked around the big table at Antonio's Restaurant and realized that all the people I cared about were here.

Across the table from us, Ms. Ludlow and her husband were laughing with my parents and with Mrs. Caris. Alan and Anne were involved in a lively discussion about her chances of getting onto the college bowl team. And Bobbie and Amanda were both playing in their ice cream and sprinkles.

Mr. Ludlow tapped his water glass with a spoon and everyone got quiet. "As you all know, we're here to celebrate," he said, "and to thank some very good friends who helped us when we needed it most."

"Mackenzie, Anne, and Mike, we're so grateful for your help in finding and returning to us our most important possession. We cannot begin to thank you enough."

He paused, and then he went on. "Sometimes, we get caught up in everyday tasks. We think we have to have that job or make this amount of money. In the process, we forget that the most important things can't be bought. Mackenzie, you've helped show us that it's better to be together than to have all the extras. I'm hoping I will see a good deal more of you, because next week I'm being transferred to a position here in Brookview where I can be with my family."

We all applauded and cheered. Amanda, who wasn't paying much attention, banged her spoon on the table.

Then Ms. Ludlow stood up. "Mrs. Caris, I especially want to thank you for helping Dan and me sort out our priorities. I'm grateful for your friendship and support." She paused and then added, "But I have to add a special thanks to someone else. Mackenzie, I want to tell you that I think the *Brookview Courier* was wrong in its choices this year. Your picture did receive honorable mention, but I still think it's a super photo." She walked around the table and stood in front of me. "Because I thought you should get a bigger award, and because you deserve more thanks than we can ever give, Dan and I would like you to have this." She put a brightly wrapped package down in front of me.

Everyone applauded as I tore into it. It was a beautiful camera. But I shook my head. "This is too much," I said, or tried to say, because I was suddenly having trouble talking.

"No, it is hardly enough to thank you for being such a wonderful second mother to Amanda," Ms. Ludlow said quietly. I think Mike and I were the only ones who heard her say that. "It was too much. I won't do that to you again. But you handled it wonderfully."

Suddenly, Mike shouted, "Take the camera, Mackenzie. We can have fun practicing taking photos together."

I liked the sound of that—together. For a moment, I remembered that once not long ago, I had wished I could be like Anne. Then I wanted to be like Ms. Ludlow. But right now, as I looked around the table at my family, at Amanda's ice cream-splattered face, and Mike's sunny grin, I was happy just being Mackenzie Tyler.

About the Author

VICTORIA M. ALTHOFF lives in a family of storytellers. She especially likes hearing, reading, and telling stories about courage and humor. She often gets ideas from her husband, David, who was the hero of her first story, and from their children, David and Christopher.

Victoria loves words. "I like to play with them, say them, roll them around on my tongue, and then make them my own." She learned this love from her father, who is a poet. She also enjoys people, especially young people. "Students I meet are vibrant, exciting, and interested in life. I'm enthusiastic for the future they will bring us," she says.

When she's not writing, Victoria works as a production editor of college textbooks. She also has been a newspaper reporter, a city planning technician, and a technical writer and editor.

At home in Columbus, Ohio, Victoria enjoys music, sports, taking walks, and reading. Her favorite books include mystery, adventure, and of course, romance